Uniform with this volume:

Hugh Hood: *The Collected Stories*

I: Flying a Red Kite

II: A Short Walk in the Rain

III: The Isolation Booth

Hugh Hood

Around the Mountain: Scenes from Montréal Life

THE COLLECTED STORIES

IV

The Porcupine's Quill, Inc.

CANADIAN CATALOGUING IN PUBLICATION DATA

Hood, Hugh, 1928-
Around the mountain: scenes from Montréal life:
the collected stories IV

ISBN 0-88984-141-1

1. Montréal (Québec) – Fiction.   I. Title.

PS8515.O49A7 1994   C813'.54   C94-932302-0
PR9199.3.H66A7 1994

Published by The Porcupine's Quill, Inc., 68 Main Street, Erin,
Ontario NOB 1TO with financial assistance from the Canada
Council and the Ontario Arts Council. The support of the Government of Ontario through the Ministry of Culture, Tourism
and Recreation is also gratefully acknowledged.

Represented in Canada by the Literary Press Group. Trade
orders available from General Distribution Services in Canada
(Toronto) and the United States (Niagara Falls). Selected titles
also available from Inland Book Company.

Cover is after a painting by Noreen Mallory.

Readied for the press by Doris Cowan.

Printed and bound by The Porcupine's Quill. The stock is
Zephyr Antique laid, and the type Galliard.

For John and Ruth Colombo with gratitude.

Contents

Author's Introduction

Around the Mountain: Scenes from Montréal Life was first published by the Toronto publishers Peter Martin Associates in a handsomely produced hardcover format in June 1967, two months after the remarkable international exposition Expo 67 opened its gates to the public. The book was intended as a documentary/fantasy portrait of the city and its people, politics, folkways, geography, and appearance. It was meant to appeal to tourists visiting the city during Expo summer, and to residents of Montréal who might wish to acquire a souvenir of those heady months more lasting than a T-shirt or stuffed animal bearing the embroidered legend 'Man and His World'. I wrote the book from mixed motives, one of them purely opportunistic. I believed naively that I might achieve a popular success.

Twenty-six years afterwards I can see that my motives for writing *Around the Mountain* were more complex than the simple attempt to produce a popular series of narratives that might at the same time be taken seriously as a work of art. The book shows its composite nature from the beginning. Maybe all works designed to represent cycles that recur regularly in the natural world necessarily reveal the intrusions of the authorial act through which the text is mediated. I thought in 1966 that I wanted to do two things. I wanted to produce a connected sequence of twelve short narratives that would form a cyclical, encyclopedic account of a dozen quarters of the city that would quite literally circle around the peak of the low hill that Montréalers call 'the mountain'. And I hoped to produce a finished work in sufficiently good time to be released to sales outlets just before Expo opened, so as to have it advertised, reviewed, and available in bookstores during the whole six-month run of the fair. I was trying to combine artistic and commercial purposes, and I didn't see anything wrong with that.

I can see now that other projects were also inscribed in the conception of *Around the Mountain*. Naturally I had an ideal reader in mind, not necessarily gender-specific but more likely a woman than a man because that's who my readers have been, then and now, women. Plus a few New Critics who might be male or female and who had been trained in the methods of close reading advocated by many teachers of literature from the 1940s through the late 1960s. Such trained readers would rejoice in the pattern of verbal cross-references that I'd deliberately embedded in my composition like a baker placing raisins in muffin dough. They might see that the name Victor Latourelle could be read as 'the winner in the little tower'.

No reader in more than a quarter of a century has ever noticed this textual detail, mentioned it to me, or referred to it in a review or critical article. Perhaps my imaginary reader wasn't to be found in this world, and the allusions that I so carefully buried in my muffin-mix may have lain in darkness all that time, perhaps only to be noticed when all the dough rises as a new leaven in the New Age.

That gives us three motives: to write a cycle of documentary/fantasies having the proportions of a calendar or a Book of Hours; to produce a commercially successful souvenir brochure for sale at Expo; to please an indefinite number of ideal readers who liked to practise New Criticism. What other elements were figured in this composite structure?

My religion makes its predictable appearance in the composition of the book. I have always been a religious believer, a Catholic by birth, upbringing, and mature conviction. While I always draw a distinction between religious conviction and ideology I realize that most secular discourse does not. Catholic belief is far from incidental to the production of *Around the Mountain*. Whether faith and dogma have here degenerated into disingenuous propaganda is a question for readers of other ideological persuasions to propose to themselves. A New Historicist might read the book as an embarrassing expression of nostalgia for a kind of thought control no longer acceptable in cultural discourse.

I made the book partly out of a series of references to the *Purgatorio* and *The Prelude*, works that if not specifically religious poems certainly represent religious experience, and even mystical experience, as an integral element of their narrative. There is some true sense in which the *Commedia*, *Paradise Lost*, and certain other long verse narratives may truthfully be described as religious poems, while *The Prelude* problematizes the notion of the religious poem. Can there be such a thing as a 'secular religious narrative poem'? That's more or less what I hoped *Around the Mountain* might turn out to be, a work that would carry on its face an innocent air of immersion in this world, the fallen secular community, so that at the crucial half-way point in the series of linked stories I could pause and transfer to humanity itself two of the attributes of the Divine Presence. 'Human purpose,' I dared to write, 'is inscrutable but undeniable.'

I wanted those acute (women) readers to take note of this transferral of the Divine to the human, and to understand that the mis/attribution was meant as part of an allusion game, that inscrutability and undeniability remain properly speaking attributes of absolute presence alone. I was then and have remained an essentialist aesthete, God help me, just the worst sort of person to be in these times.

Wordsworth wound *The Prelude* up to the top of Mount Snowdon; the progress of the poem is clear, from the surface and shores of the lake to the mountaintop. And there he imagines he can rest, ready for the vision of the heavenly city documented at the end of the second book of *The Excursion*. Much recent writing on this poet insists that the winding up is accompanied by a simultaneous winding down, a deeply depressive conviction in the text that when we reach the mountaintop there is no place to go but down. The mountaintop vision comes at the exact centre of the text of *Around the Mountain*, and afterwards it's downhill all the way back to the menacing surface of Lac des Deux Montagnes. What goes up must come down.

Two final motives, collaborative and celebratory. I haven't often collaborated in work with another artist, but *Around the Mountain* was rooted in the close friendship I had formed with the painter Seymour Segal, who is represented by name in the opening story, 'Seymour the goalie'. The representation of a person or thing that 'really exists' is absolutely never the same as the person or thing in themselves. A representation is itself, and not something else. I introduced Seymour the goalie in a kind of authorial superstition, a certificate that my book was real itself, and concerned with real people and things.

The opening story signalled a formal design meant to control the work from first to last. 'Snow!' Winter in Montréal is long and hard. As Coleridge says, 'the spring comes slowly up this way'. This snowy book continually plays with representations of reality, but the most pressingly real persons in the stories invariably turn out to be purely fictitious. Victor Latourelle of 'The Village Inside' or Thierry Desautels of 'A Green Child' seem more real to me and, I suspect, to most readers, than Seymour the goalie. The magic trick of fictive discovery. Seymour was in the book as a sign of our intention to collaborate with one another. When John Robert Colombo, our editor, persuaded Peter Martin that it would be a good idea to publish the book, he proposed it as a guide to Montréal, with illustrations to be provided by Seymour. Two of the stories were accompanied by Seymour's drawings when they appeared in the short-lived Montréal magazine *Parallel*. 'Around Theatres' was illustrated by three drawings, 'Starting Again on Sherbrooke Street' by one, a vivid rendering of the principal character in the story.

It is surprising to see how little realistic and how imaginative these illustrations are. They are definitely Seymour Segal renderings, in no way surreal but not in the least subordinate to my text. I was surprised when I saw them for the first time. I considered them out of harmony with my words, but the passage of a quarter of a century has persuaded me that the painter saw deeply into my intentions. The drawings are pretty dark, even ominous.

Our collaboration came to a disastrous end not long after Peter Martin agreed to the conception of an illustrated work. Seymour was badly injured in a hockey accident and full collaboration had to be deferred for more than a dozen years. We published *Scoring: Seymour Segal's art of hockey* as a collaboration in 1979. Seymour, as his name might suggest, could see things that I couldn't see immediately. He knew that the stories in *Around the Mountain* were not the sunny optimistic anecdotes that some people have found them, ornamented with a glittering style and the surface charms of rhythm and intricate syntax.

'Human purpose is inscrutable but undeniable,' well, maybe. I thought so then. I'm not so sure now.

That rather flippant transferral of the Divine into the human appears on page 94 of the original printed text, at the exact mid-point of the collection. I can remember congratulating myself on the precision of this placement. In some interview or other I seem to have said that this was the holiest moment in the book. You could step from there into the next world.

But which next world? There are at least four of them: Hell and Heaven, to say nothing of Purgatory and Limbo. I use the language of Christian teleology here because the book insists on it. The top of the mountain is the place where heroic and/or Divine transactions take place, Sinai, Olivet, Calvary. I had a dim awareness as I wrote that what I had done in the first six stories was to elevate my narrative towards a great celebration. This was the last and most urgent of the forces in my imagination that led me towards the invention of a complex work. A souvenir brochure, sure. A money-maker perhaps, a book for a small group of close readers, a friendly collaboration, all those things, but a celebration before anything else.

Celebration must be the principal object of prayer. There is petitionary prayer, the most often practised form, and there are the prayers of thanksgiving and contrition, admirable under-takings, but the great central form is that of celebration of the way the heavens declare the glory of God. 'Look at the creation, see how it is made, how wonderfully, how marvellously.' This is the intention of the metaphysics of *presence* so strongly repudi-ated by contemporary thought. *Around the Mountain* is a book against deconstruction, written in 1966 when deconstruction had scarcely been heard of. Events overtake books just as they do politicians and generals. It is perfectly possible to decon-struct the text of *Around the Mountain*, to show that it isn't the joyfully affirmative work of secular/religious narrative that I thought it was twenty-six years ago. In this essay I may give the impression that the book should now be read in this way, but that would be a mistaken reading.

Where I went wrong in my writing of the book was in mak-ing rather too prominent the sunlit high points in the design, which are fewer than I realized. The most pressing, *present* scenes in the work take place in darkness. Perhaps 'Light Shining out of Darkness' which is the title of the February story, is the right title for the entire work. Perhaps I should have called it that instead of *Around the Mountain* but the intentions of the two phrases are identical. Denial of the metaphysics of presence leaves us totally in the dark; there can be no question of light showing through. But such a denial would be the enemy of my narrative; most of the best bits take place in darkness mitigated by deep light. The vision of the green child, the ascent of the staircase to the gypsy hideaway, the union of Gilles O'Neill and Denise Gariépy, certain late-night adventures along Mill Street in the docks area, the transformation of the 'afternoon of great splendour' into the menace of the book's closing paragraph, the oncoming darkness of the most effective of the stories, 'The Village Inside'. It is through this falling, spreading darkness that the light must shine, if it is to shine at all.

All this is not to deny that the ordinary necessities of literary invention are strictly observed. The stories have definite rhetorical intentions. I don't dismiss the 'surface effects' as accidental and valueless; they are the first things the reader encounters. I meant to make the book as full of surface design as possible. The first and most obvious element is the mixed language in which I wrote. English, yes, but a continually varying level of style and frequent interpolations of French words, phrases, even whole sentences, I would have liked to produce a fully bilingual work, something like the writing of Gail Scott, but the attempt would have overstrained my linguistic resources. I could not have managed extended passages in the French of Québec, and had to make do with infrequent bits of dialogue, sometimes quoted directly from newspapers.

> '*Un autre samedi de la matraque!*'
> '*Salauds Gestapos!*'

Many Québecers will recall the original *samedi de la matraque,* a sad incident in the political life of the sixties in the province. '*Matraque*' isn't a bit of Québécois argot; it can be found in Harrap or Larousse, and it means 'nightstick', 'billy club' or 'truncheon'. I used 'nightstick' as the English

equivalent in the story 'One Way North and South' because less
discomforting than its synonyms.

The problem of the linguistic representation of a bilingual
social situation is a very difficult one for a writer who knows the
two languages in question but feels incompetent to write literary prose in her or his second language. The best I could do was
to ensure the authenticity of the French utterances in the stories
by taking them word for word from French newspapers or
from shop windows or the popular songs of the day. When
Stéphane Dérôme leaves Marie-Ange behind on his departure
for Paris, she appeals to him in the words of Jacques Brel – *'Ne
me quitte pas.'*

And her boyfriend replies, 'Brel,' to indicate that he is aware
of her source. 'Don't leave me!' she begs, in the words of a musical hit. But Stéphane feels, perhaps rightly, that there is much
role-playing affectation in Marie-Ange's self-portrayal as the
abandoned *amante*. The story is called 'Bicultural Angela' and
its heroine impressed me so much that she became a principal
character in the 1970 novel *A Game of Touch* and continued to
appear in my later stories, particularly those set in the imaginary
town of Stoverville, Ontario. In *The Motor Boys in Ottawa*, my
novel of 1986, the reader finds Marie-Ange safely back in
Stoverville, married to Duncan McCallum and living under her
baptismal names of Angela Mary. I chose the name Angela to
suggest her status of messenger or go-between (Gk.
angelos/messenger) in the Canadian bilingual situation. Her
story, the third in *Around the Mountain*, the March story, is
placed in that position because of the tempestuous windy
weather characteristic of the vernal equinox. The whole book is
full of weather. For Marie-Ange Robinson 'the pale watery haze
of early March, the snow melting, evaporating, obscuring the
weak sun' is a paradigm of her Montréal adventures, pale, weak,
obscured. The snow of the beginning and ending of the cycle is
here divided into three states, solid, liquid, gaseous. Marie-
Ange finds it difficult to make her way through the half-
perceptions of cultural difference she has acquired. In the end
she is dumped by the dubiously authentic chansonnier. '"Brel,"
said Stéphane absently, and he turned away.'

The adverb 'absently' tells what my narrator makes of the

situation. The supposedly authentic voice of Québec group-awareness withdraws from the naive advances of the messenger from Stoverville. I feel badly about this but I didn't design the society that gave me my text. Marie-Ange Robinson absolutely never captures Stéphane Dérôme. Her fate is the speedy, strong Scot – McCallum. There is nothing to be done about that.

At the level of its cosmetic surface structure then, the work was contrived and polished in the smallest detail. Reading it now I remember the city as it struck me during my first four or five years there, fascinating, swarming with suggestive details like the possibility of endless linguistic joking. At the extreme east end of the city in 1966 there lay a street in a new subdivision called rue Valdombre. Imagine my delight when I found it at the end of the 95 busline and realized that it was the street of the valley of the shadow, and that a gross excavation, a deep depression in the ground, lay next to it. The street names wrote the story, Valdombre, Lacordaire, d'Avila. In this text from the edge, when the main character in the September story 'A Green Child' prepares for bed he takes a long look from his window at 'the vast stretches of obscurity outside', which are relieved only by 'the brave lights of a few new duplexes on rue d'Avila, a hundred feet of brand-new street almost buried in the darkness'. The documents of the local scene wrote the story.

When I imagined Thierry Desautels (of the altars, *autels*) merging into the dark I was moved towards a new way of writing, and I interpolated into 'A Green Child' a brief, four-paragraph essay, separated from the rest of the story by double-spacing. This is the passage, much commented on afterwards, that begins, 'An image recurrent in the work of modern film-makers, especially in that of Antonioni, is justified in actual life by the appearance of this part of town.' The voice goes on to remark that, 'The effect is as if history were running backwards; instead of these buildings seeming the heralds of stunning development, of a new age, they seem under Antonioni's harsh inspection to be the ruined monuments of a past describable now only by archaeological investigation.'

This passage, written in May 1966, is the first specific reference in my work to 'a new age.' And the whole passage is the first instance of essayistic interpolation in narrative of a kind that I've used again and again in the books known collectively as *The New Age/Le nouveau siècle*. Because of these historiographical underpinnings the story was surpassingly easy to write; it came to life like a wriggling serpent, some Québécoise Mélusine, under my fingers, and predicted much of my next three decades of work. The future was already there in the percept of history running backwards, so that *the future predicted the past*. Twenty-six years later, if you travel to the site of rue Valdombre you will find it recoverable only by archaeological investigation. The years have overbuilt it.

This is the reverse process to that which created 'The Village Inside'. In 'A Green Child' time has buried the valley of the shadow under a new city; in 'The Village Inside' time lays darkness bare. Victor Latourelle's nineteenth-century village and farmstead have been stripped naked and flattened into the image of a monumental parking lot. Thierry Desautels' dark valley has been buried beneath the encroachments of urban sprawl. From being the extreme edge of town in 1966, the district is now practically downtown, the edge of development having moved ten miles further east. History seems to be winding its spools in opposite directions, clockwise and counterclockwise, in the east and west ends of the same city. This is what I mean by suggesting that chronology doesn't always run in the same direction. In different parts of a given city (especially if the city is a purely literary invention) chronology and history may function in quite opposite ways, with here the past looming up ever more insistently in the group consciousness, and there the future stripping the group of its awareness of the past. Different groups: different stories.

So we mourn, quite conventionally, the disappearance of the green farmstead under the miles of asphalt and the colossal malls, but we haven't learned to mourn the real-estate development buried under a dozen newer, larger developments. The present in the story 'A Green Child' that seemed so new and menacing in 1966 has vanished under the press of newer times; the mall developers and the cranes and the cement-mixers have taken themselves eastward from Eden. The new has turned into the familiar, the spool has unwound.

I'm not an historiographer, not a sociologist, and I would

make no claim to authoritative wisdom as an analyst of social trends. But I would confess that I intended to create an encyclopedic record of the city as it was in 1966/1967, that would enshrine an historical moment like the proverbial fly in amber. I wanted to give a kind of fossil-like existence to something that was in process of being born and simultaneously passing away. It is fascinating to me to go through these twelve stories to judge what has remained in place and what has been swept away and forgotten. Every reader who knows Montréal will have an opinion about this. But some things have remained unmistakably in place.

The weather's the same. If I were writing the book this year, it would still begin and end with the word 'snow'. The early darkness of a northerly town in winter would find its way into any present or future narrative presentation of Montréal. So would the mist. I'm astonished to see how much I'd insisted on mistiness, indistinctness of vision, at key moments of the work, especially in the closing passages of the last story. Nothing less than some major climatic shift, the melting of the polar ice caps or final disappearance of the ozone layer, will cause my description of a damp Christmas afternoon to be superseded. Geography and climate have remained constant and so have their literary uses.

> A breeze stirred, slightly thinning the mist, wrapping swirls of vapour around the lonely black figure; all at once the scene composed itself into meaning. Everything in my range of vision was obscured by mist, except those agitated thin black limbs. I raised my eyes to the sources of the river, several miles westwards where the lake contracts. Shore, water, air, were all enveloped and changed, the city inexistent. Far off northwest, the high hills rose ghostly from the melting ice and snow.

When I wrote the end of 'The River Behind Things' I was trying to resolve the old, vexed question about the difference between symbolism and allegory. This may not be the place to raise one of the fundamental problems in the theory of literature, so I'll simply note that the title 'The River Behind Things' begs the reader to mark out other levels of meaning than those given in the bald story line. This *isn't just* a story about a man who drives out to look at the river on a wet Christmas afternoon. It's somehow or other a discussion of the links between the movement of time and the permanence of things, deep temporality, to use the term of Paul Ricoeur. But how can a single narrative tell multiple stories simultaneously?

My December mist is not just physical mist; the damp is damper than the damps of December. The thin agitated black figure is an all too familiar visitant. Him and his long black rod or pole! The text offers a multiplicity of meanings, but how is this managed? I would propose that I had used the conventional methods of allegory known to Dante and accurately described by him, but pre-existing his time perhaps by centuries. Allegory is precise and definite in its linings-out of modes of signifying. Symbolism is vague, a matter of hints and winks and nudges. Know what I mean? Know what I mean? The symbolist delivers less than meets the eye and ear, the allegorist more. When I use the words 'I raised my eyes to the source of the river', I mean my reader to remember some such words as 'I will lift mine eyes unto the Lord'. I'm invoking an absolute reality.

An absolute and *present*, the practice of the presence of God. An anagogical real, the highest stretch of literary action. My book was meant to work along the lines of Christian allegory named by Dante in the letter to Can Grande della Scala. For any scriptural text, and likewise for any artfully formed poetic text, there are four legitimate levels of interpretation: literal, moral/tropological, allegorical, anagogical. For example, the creative words 'Let there be light' may be understood *literally* to describe the beginnings of natural light at the dawn of Creation. Their *moral/tropological* sense describes the human feelings and intelligence as enlightened by the presence of Christ. Their *allegorical* sense teaches us that Christ is perpetually born anew in His Church. The *anagogical* sense, the highest reach of signification, describes the carrying of the immortal soul to glory, by and in Christ.

I haven't worked out all four levels of signification for every incident in *Around the Mountain*, but I would claim that the *literal* narrative is always clear and definite and the *anagogical* implication reasonably obvious. We know exactly where we are at any given moment in the twelve stories, and we have a good notion of what is finally being implied. But it is open to any analyst of a different school of interpretation to propose a rival view, a totally different system of levels of meaning.

'The high hills rose ghostly from the melting ice and snow.' I know what I meant to imply by that image, the recesses and secret places of Beatitude. The melting, changing forms of solids, ice and snow, turn into the impalpable, and the Holy Ghost is present in them. But a psychoanalytically oriented critic is perfectly empowered to observe that the vision of a vast, curvilinear, indistinct, milky surface, is retained by those of us who were fed at the breast, from the earliest moments of infancy. I, who yield to nobody in my admiration of the female breast, must concede that a primordial image of that sort may have been present when the end of the book was writing me. I am told that similar images are often lodged in the foundations of mystical experience. Certainly there is something godly about the breast. The two types of image, mystical and infantile, must lie close together in most mature imagining.

So the book starts and finishes in misty obscurity and snow; the high hills rose ghostly from melting ice and snow on that Christmas afternoon when Mary first suckled Jesus. But the cycle of the year is never final and the book begins its seasonal rotation on its opening page which flows out of this closing. Successive Christmases overlap in the book, as indeed they seem to do in life, as one grows older and the years spin faster. I meant the end and the beginning of the book to merge into a sempiternal wintriness, while at the same time the opening story, 'The Sportive Centre of Saint Vincent de Paul', had to serve as my January narrative, an account that looks backwards and forwards like the statues of Janus, the Roman god of the New Year. This opening story begins before the moment of the birth of Christ and ends three weeks afterwards, well into the next year. It is concerned with the misadventures of a convivial defenceman called Fred Carpenter – the surname makes another of those allusions that people never notice – who is made the scapegoat for a lost hockey game by the narrator and his friend Seymour the goalie. The reader is supposed to notice a number of Christological allusions. The season is Christmas/New Year's. The scapegoat is called Carpenter. There is an insistence on the heroic mythology of hockey that circles around the enchanted figure of Maurice Richard. 'He could score on the Devil himself. If Maurice was dying and the goalie gave him the angle, he'd get up and score.' Social mythology merges with legend very explicitly when the narrator refers to 'the little door that might lead to the building superintendent's office.' Strait is the gate and narrow. This bald description introduces a documentary observation. '... over it stands a big grey plaster statue of the Blessed Virgin with the Child in her arms; the statue has a circular electric halo. It all fits in.'

In that arena in that month of 1966 there *was* a statue of the Virgin and Child with an electric halo at the top. My words 'the building superintendent' refer to the supreme authority principle at every interpretive level, from the building manager to Almighty God. The language doesn't have to be specially elegant if the context is O K. It all fits in: 'the Virgin and Child', the season, the Carpenter.

I had twelve months to incorporate in my cycle, and four seasons. The book is composed of four units of three stories each; one of my tasks was to fit the stories to the months in which they took place. You have to put your December/January story in a hockey arena, but where does the February story go? Why does the country of the *ruelles*, as described in 'Light Shining out of Darkness', seem so evocative of deep deep freeze and February isolation? The cue, which seems so necessary to my imagination, was in this case the social reality that most of the dwellings in *ruelle* country were separated from each other and rented unheated. The tenant supplied his own heating device in those days, often a dangerous oil-fired space-heater. Chill and isolation seemed the essentials of February life; they are the keys to 'Light Shining out of Darkness'. When you ascend the dangerous and icy outside staircase that leads to the house of Tom, King of the Gypsies, you don't know what you are about to see. The door opens and you are almost supernaturally confronted by 'a rich, mixed impression of much pale electric light in which were splashed patch after patch of brilliant colour, high up in the room'. These polyvalent impressions bring to the narrator an intense, almost religious experience. 'I was mysteriously overwhelmed by this various and splendid sight with feelings of a hidden and immense joy.' The passage is put forward by the narrator as a Wordsworthian comment on the possibilities of 'a rounded period in the life of the imagination'. There is explicit dependence on the literary procedures of the secular/religious poem, in this case, Book XII of *The Prelude*.

Observable reality, the furnishings of a hockey arena in 1966, or of a self-contained, unheated, coldwater apartment in a crowded midtown district in the same year, is merged with purely invented matter. 'They smiled, and began to sing sweetly to their mother, an old song in the minor about the larks in wintertime.' I inserted the singing and the song into the texture of the narration, in order to prepare the narrator's departure. 'Avenue de Chateaubriand grows deadly cold after midnight in February.' The magical incident is irrecoverable because its agents have moved on like the gypsies they are.

The March story, chilly and unpromising, is about the change in the seasons, emergence into equinoctial gale from the iron cold of February. Angela Mary Robinson, a personage who appears in several of my books, plans to resolve certain eternal disputes in her role of angelic messenger. She comes to the far east of the city, a solidly French district, with her bicultural message of love and understanding that nobody ever understands. Hers is a tale full of chilly cross-currents approaching gale force. The setting is full of the associations of the east wind, characterless except for its flatness and lack of charm. The narrative voice specifies the light. 'The pale watery haze of early March, the snow melting, evaporating, obscuring the weak sun.' So much for Marie-Ange's diplomatic functions.

I wonder where George Tabah is now. I remember him so vividly in his incarnation as proprietor of the Montrose Record Centre, 'on Bélanger, west of Montée Saint-Michel'. You could walk or drive to the spot with perfect ease, given these precise directions; the book really is a reader's guide to the intersection of time and space. I'm continually mystified by its insistence on the actual. I confessed to George Tabah, whom I knew well in

another context, that I'd 'put him in a book', which of course is
an impossible action. George was a pretty unflappable fellow,
and wasn't bothered by this revelation. He seemed incurious
about what I might have written, may have disbelieved in the
whole enterprise. When I told him his place was the most exciting record store in town he was more interested and made the
remark I've quoted in the story, 'I may use that in an ad.' I don't
know that he ever did.

A flourishing record store in the east end, patronized by the
recording stars of the city as well as by their admirers, struck me
as the perfect background for the story of Marie-Ange, a
woman determined to make a place for herself at the centre of
the francophone arts and entertainment world of the day, an
unheard-of venture that might accurately represent the end of a
long freeze-up. I saw the story as a romance of late winter and
early spring, with the twist at the end of Stéphane's departure
for a warmer climate. 'The March light was extremely ambiguous, very pale, chilly looking … it was still plenty cold out, but
another few weeks would see us out of it. The equinoctial gales,
very troublesome in Montréal, had just begun, and the wind
was gusting to fifty.' I sit at my desk today, writing this introduction at the end of September in 1993, and the equinoctial
gales of early fall are in full swing, the wind outside my room
gusting precisely to fifty, and not fifty kilometres but fifty *miles*
per hour, gale force on the Beaufort scale. Perhaps the greatest
index of permanence is the weather. Taxes, lovemaking,
weather, the three greatest subjects of human conversation, and
the greatest of these is the weather, which everybody discusses
and nobody does anything about.

Around the Mountain tries to do something about the
weather. If it doesn't enshrine the equinoctial gales, it makes a
fuss about them and preserves our awareness of them for
decades. Less permanent aspects of our society have perished
utterly in the long years since I wrote this book, but the weather
goes on blowing. The story 'Around Theatres', planned as a
story of early spring, and its immediate successor, 'Le grand
déménagement', a history of a May Day institution, have both
dated so distinctly as to have the air of historical fiction. In
'Around Theatres' I chose somewhat arbitrarily to link spring-

time with the acting profession, the stage and films. I provided a catalogue of filming and film-going activity in the city during the mid-1960s, trying to suggest the impression of some great cultural expression. After winter is over, around Easter, you stop watching hockey and switch to going to the movies. History has invalidated this observation; the Stanley Cup playoffs now continue into the second week of June!!. The story kept doubling back on me like kinky barbed wire. I tried to link films and live theatre in my account of the problems of Gus Delahaye, promising young actor unable to live by the exercise of his talent. Spring kept turning into frustrated and embittered fall. Placed in a situation requiring improvisatory gifts, Gus can't invent anything. His talent fails him at the moment of truth and in exasperation at his own lack of invention he exclaims to the narrator, 'So you're one of those saps that lets the weather affect you? Christ, man, the weather isn't good or bad, that's simply the pathetic fallacy, don't you even know that … the universe doesn't give a damn about you … besides, God is dead.'

The account of the cinema of the period and the predicament of the perpetually unemployed actor have an inescapably dated look, most of the films mentioned lost in oblivion, the actor having turned permanently to cab-driving as a means of livelihood. The action of the narration seems as remote as anything in *Gone With the Wind*. The wind blows the ephemeral persons and institutions away. The movies of the mid-sixties are as forgotten as the custom of Moving Day pictured in my romance of mid-spring, 'Le grand déménagement'. The custom lapsed some fifteen years ago. April 30th is no longer Moving Day. The game of musical chairs, in which a last solitary lessee might find himself homeless, no longer goes on. Economic decline has hit the city; the market for apartment housing has collapsed. You can move when and where you wish; the market is so poor that leases have ceased to have much force. The economic basis of the housing market has been so drastically undermined that I wouldn't think of writing a story about Moving Day now. 'Le grand déménagement' has been altered by time into historical fiction; its mid-spring charm seems faded and bittersweet.

That hasn't happened to 'Looking Down From Above'. This story, the allegorical centre and holiest place in the sequence, begins with a prayerful declaration. 'Fair weather implies heightened perception in my book.' This is to be a story of June moving into July.

> Summer is short in Montréal, and even in late June you some-
> times get a day which is autumnal in tone, where the colour of
> the sky seems to bring out the soft browns and dark reds from
> the crowded trunks and branches in the woods. You might call
> it the autumn of summer's first pulse.

This interjection describes the weather on Saint-Jean Baptiste Day, in the imaginary year of the story. 'There was a solemn stillness about it,' as indeed there should be on the great national festival of Québec, June 24th. The great precursor of the Messiah, the enemy of Herod and victim of Salome, John seems the appropriate figure to preside over this solemn time when the narrator climbs to the highest point in his range of vision and transfers the inscrutable but undeniable from the Divine to the human. 'It looked from where I stood as if you could step in a single stride onto the edge of the runway, or into the next world.'

You could launch yourself from here into eternity. The voice of the speaker now seems to be haunted by an underlying dubiety. Human purpose may be undeniable, but may it not also be misdirected? I would qualify the optimism placed at the centre of the text by words that suggest more recent, second and third, reflections.

And I notice in the two following 'summer' stories, 'One Way North and South' and 'The Village Inside', that a certain double optic has since intruded on the actions shown at the original time of writing. The July story opens with the prose poem that celebrates the marvellous variety of the city's parks. The text gives the names of twenty parks in all parts of the city on its first page, and then focuses on the central location, Parc Lafontaine, identifying it as a lifesaver. Now the story deviates alarmingly into an account of the sometimes violent political manifestations of the epoch, which often took place in this very park. High pastoral summer becomes the backdrop for contestations between police and demonstrators, with blows being exchanged and blood shed.

Parc Lafontaine, we learn, lies just north of *un des quartiers les plus déshérités de la métropole*,' almost a slum, the south-central district of the aging inner city, a natural breeding ground for a revolutionary sense of oppression; there are some assured sociological judgements interpolated here. Then a young man and woman step forward and act out their roles of peaceful compromise, the foundation of happy marriage. The weather presides. 'When there is a breeze, as is usual in this city, the trees are full of a soft rushing breathy sound.' We can identify this sound as the whispering of the Holy Spirit, the correspondent breeze of the opening lines of *The Prelude*. 'One Way North and South' benefits (or suffers) from its double optic as much as a narrative can without collapsing into formlessness.

Fragmented collapse doesn't threaten the following two stories. They are arguably the two most coherent and successful artistic structures in the book. Between them they skew the line of the narrative as summer deepens to fall. They are both ghost stories in which apparitions of people and places haunt the central characters, Victor Latourelle and Thierry Desautels.

Victor Latourelle, the winner in the little tower, is haunted, as so many of us in the late twentieth century are haunted, by the past. Not the very remote past, many centuries ago, but the familiar past extending back a century and a quarter to the time when our great-grandparents were children, the 1860s and 1870s. The farmstead buried under blacktop, the traceable old village inside the suburban growth, these are the remembered past that gives the title to the story, 'The Village Inside'. Such a past is embedded in the memories of many Europeans and North Americans. I have to adopt a Eurocentric posture because I know nothing about Africa or Asia or Oceania. The culture-memories of Tibetans and Vietnamese are certainly unlike ours; they may not be tinctured by recollections of the village inside. But most of us in the West are troubled by its fictitious, dreamed tranquillity. This has helped to make the story accessible to its readers. Like Victor Latourelle, we too sit alone through the oncoming dark, cherishing our hallucinations. Can you blame us?

The September symbolic structure, 'A Green Child', gives the book its definitive downwards turn. It is the only story in the book that is narrated wholly impersonally; there are no references to a first-person narrator. Thierry Desautels is strictly on his own during his weird searchings through a time sequence that sometimes spins backwards. He is identified in the first line of the story as *un vrai jusqu'auboutist*, a traveller who will go right to the very end of things. He rides the 95 bus straight to the edge of town, to the terminus of the run, and there he begins a flirtation with non-existence. He pursues a mysterious apparition, the green child of the title, into the valley of the shadow.

This valley of depression strangely resembles Stonehenge, or some other of those collections of monuments so ancient that their use and meaning are lost to us. In Thierry's case, the indecipherable monuments are not relics of a long distant, haunting past, but *relics of the future*, the uncompleted ramps and overpasses of a monstrous cloverleaf, half buried in construction workers' detritus, mud, garbage, the desert monoliths of the Montée de Saint-Léonard interchange. They are the heralds of a civilization that has died before its beginnings. Thierry loses his way as he tries to follow the track of the goddess of this place. As the story turns finally into a tale of haunting, he lifts his head a last time to stare at a figure on a massive concrete slab rising before him. 'On it was some ghastly design.' We don't know what these immensely futuric constructions will have been used for but ritual execution will very likely have taken place on such sites. Thierry's surname, Desautels, means 'of the altars' and we can infer that the open end of the story will allow him no final escape.

The closing stories work around towards the opening of the work; they deal with autumn and early winter. 'Starting Again on Sherbrooke Street' begins as a narrative of the strictest autobiography. In 1966 I owned a Volkswagen bus which was then reaching the end of its useful life. It is portrayed in 'The Sportive Centre of Saint Vincent de Paul' and again in 'Le grand déménagement' and then it drops out of the narrative, as it did from my life. I exchanged the rusted-out vehicle for a brand-new, bright green Volkswagen beetle.

'Why'd you sell your bus?'

'The bottom fell out, you know that.'

Those are the true voices of Seymour Segal and Hugh Hood. The attempt to carry eighteen canvases to a Sherbrooke Street gallery from a distant studio took place almost exactly as I have depicted it. It is the 'almost' that divides fiction from reporting or direct witness. The incident exists in the fiction purely as a comic introduction to a story of mid-autumn, the resumption of the hockey season at the Forum and the narrator's contacts with the conniving Chris Holt, who sometimes escorts his wife to the arena for the game, and sometimes another lady whom he describes to his wife as his uncle. Sometimes he brings neither woman to the game, in which case his extra ticket is available for the narrator, supposedly Hugh Hood who has so many story ideas that he won't live to write them. The comic/ironic action works itself out according to the availability of this floating season ticket. If Christopher's love life is going well, the narrator has to buy himself a standing-room ticket. Intrigues of this kind have been carried on in crowded hockey arenas since there have been such places to squeeze into. A quintessentially autumnal tale. Christopher goes back to his wife, and now in October he is taking a fresh grip on things; the second season ticket is not available this season. Christopher strolls off to the Ritz, full of assurance. The street, the story and the man are neatly aligned.

'Predictions of Ice' needn't detain us long; the nature of the story is plain from its title. This is the second place in the work where the simmering political unrest characteristic of great port cities, Hamburg, New York, Venice, is allowed to surface. The misery is always there beneath the skin, one of the points I tried to make, as unobtrusively as possible, in the book. If the reader wants to see it as a chronicle of unrest and oppression, she or he has a perfect justification for doing so. There is always trouble on the docks. *Les débardeurs sont en grève*. Even with the coming of highly sophisticated loading/ unloading equipment, dockworkers still feel the injustice of their situation, perhaps will always do so. They are frozen in an inescapable cycle of layoff/hiring/layoff. 'There's been a lot of opposition to this deal,' says an analyst of the situation, 'political opposition, union opposition, commercial discontent.' He might as well be describing the Free Trade deal of the nineties. The December cold comes on; the ice thickens visibly; the narrator announces the end of the year.

And then, as things end, with the river and the mist behind things, everything starts up again. The Christmas of one year merges into the Christmas of the next. At the winter solstice, the very dark time, there is nevertheless a prospect of widening light. I thought that this might be the motto of the whole work, 'Light Shining out of Darkness.' I may have been wrong, as the author of a book is always wrong about it until she or he learns to read it right. We are taught today that the only truth about reading is that there are no true readings, only an interminable series of versions of the story. The living author cries, 'I knew what I meant when I wrote that,' and a quarter of a century later, turning himself into a new reader, feels separated from himself as writer, uncertain of those first shadowy revelations, perhaps a little bit self-deconstructed. But that is only a fleeting trace of an impression; the author knows what he meant, doesn't he?

* * *

I am grateful for the opportunity to restore the surname of the original dedicatees of *Around the Mountain* to its proper place. It was inadvertently omitted in the earlier editions. The book has always been 'For John and Ruth Colombo, with gratitude.'

Around the Mountain

The Sportive Centre of Saint Vincent de Paul

SNOW. MOIST, HEAVY, fat flakes melting as they hit, down your coat collar, in your boots, underfoot, piling up in eaves-troughs and on outdoors Christmas trees, shorting their ice-blue, silver, yellow, and red strands of light. Snow everywhere this mid-December, not a heavy fall this time – we haven't had much yet – but irksome on Friday night at six-fifteen because of the traffic. If snow, then snow-removal equipment and crews, the salt trucks lugging slowly up the hill on Van Horne, growl-ing in low gear. Whish ... whish ... whoosh ... the salt tumbles out behind in crystals, melts, and electrolizes the body metal of fifty thousand cars.

When we got into the car that Friday night, the windows clouded over immediately, and we both began to swear as we threw the goalie equipment and my kitbag and skates into the back, conscious of the half-hour drive ahead, and wondering how long it would take to traverse the level crossing on Rock-land. I spun the wheels backing away from the garage, which made Seymour, the goalie, turn and stare at me.

'Gotta do it in second.'

We sunfished up the driveway. After two minutes in the car, our breath made it impossible to see out. I hate cold weather, even moderate cold, so I usually keep the windows shut, but a little cold air on the glass works wonders, so I nodded when Seymour glanced at me.

'All right, open the damn things.' We went down the street, around the corner, and hit bad traffic as soon as we tried to get onto Rockland; we were a couple of hundred yards short of the level crossing, just by the park, and the bells were ringing, the red lights swinging, the combined efforts of two wealthy subur-ban municipalities, Outremont and the Town of Mount Royal, having succeeded for years in denying the plain public interest of the rest of Montréal. They don't want anything done to the level crossing that will increase heavy traffic on Rockland, so to the detriment of the needs of the citizenry in general, they have put off from one year to the next the creation of an overpass or underpass, from planning council to engineering study, until the issue has evolved from scandal to joke to folklore.

They claim they're going to do something about it next summer, but I'll believe that when I see it.

Only ten minutes to get across this time, though, and from Rockland to L'Acadie, where we turned north towards the Metropolitan, was another five minutes. Half the time for the ride out of town spent on the first half-mile, such is the obduracy of the flourishing suburbanite.

Sometimes, working my way along beside the park towards the level crossing in winter twilight or blackness, I used to have an infernal vision of the place as an immense and horrid ashpit. There are piles of ashes and discarded rubbers, old tires, dead cats, at the back of the park where the snow-removal men heap tumuli of grey slush to await the coming of spring. It seemed ashy, grey to black, infinite, that stretch of obscurity along the railroad right-of-way, where now and then a truck might be seen, its body tilted at a dangerous angle. Spectral muffled figures prodded at lumps of packed snow and ordure as one came by; it was always mysteriously saddening to observe their dauntless activity.

Not too bad on L'Acadie, a bit of a tie-up trying to get into the far right lane for the Metropolitan turnoff, but after fifty cars had passed on my right somebody finally slowed and waved me on. I don't think he saw my grateful salute because my car, a degraded Volkswagen bus, allows of little visibility in or out from abaft the beam. We pulled up to the green arrow and headed east, neither of us with much to say, concentrating on the coming game.

Seymour won't eat before a game. He takes a light lunch about two-thirty and dines afterwards, natural in a goal-keeper, I suppose, whose tensions are great. I play defence, and Seymour makes me look good or bad depending, so I can perhaps afford to do as I do and eat around five-thirty. After the game we have drinks and sandwiches. We don't talk much on the way out; that comes later.

'You left the front of the net on their second goal.'

'I did, hell. Polsky should have been there; the play came in on my side.'

'Anyway, don't keep doing it.'

We play in an informal two-team league, the Sportsman's League, organized a dozen years ago by some men who had played hockey all their lives and wanted to keep up with it as they got into their late twenties and early thirties. There is one strict rule: no board checking. There's a seasonal series of twenty-five games, and scoring records are kept; we have an elaborate and convivial end-of-the-season dinner. There must be lots of leagues like this, and some of the men in them play in higher-class leagues as well. Seymour plays three nights a week, once with us and twice in the Town of Mount Royal Senior, where there are some really good players.

'Shibley has taken up curling Friday nights,' mumbled Seymour. 'Curling!'

I eased up the ramp onto the Metropolitan and at once began to drive as fast as possible, which isn't all that fast. We crept up to fifty-five and the bus began to shudder a bit in the wind, always strong on the elevated highway. I couldn't get over fifty-six or seven, but that speed will heat the car slightly, and I got much better vision as our breath stopped condensing on the windows.

Past Place Crémazie, spic and span in black and white and grey brick, all lit up for the Friday night shoppers. Past a parish church of daringly advanced design, its big front window radiating pale yellow and apple-green bars of light over the snow. Over and past myriads of streaking lights. Then a wide sweeping turn coming down towards Saint-Hubert and Christophe-Colomb, whizzing on towards D'Iberville and at last Pie-IX, pronounced 'peanoof'. I looked at my watch as we came down off the Metro.

'Quarter to seven.'

'I've got my equipment anyway,' said Seymour. 'I can dress in plenty of time.' It takes him around twenty minutes to get it all on; he has pads for very unusual parts of the body, and rightly so. His face-mask, a strange plastic structure of his own design, closely resembles the death-mask of Keats. He said, 'We'll be there before seven,' as we took a right onto Pie-IX.

Here the prospect of the city changes as you go north, heading off the island. The lights of the Metropolitan recede, a pale

stippled line away behind to the west. On your left there's nothing but dark space belonging to Saint-Michel de Laval, half-
developed industrial park, I think, with spur lines jutting off
into fields, and here and there an occasional abandoned boxcar,
and a taxi park or gas station. Pie-IX was just a ribbon development a few years ago, but now there is beginning to be a bit of a
spread eastwards towards Ville de Saint-Léonard. There are
Dairy Queens closed for the winter, on our right, and used-car
lots, small restaurants and raw new shopping centres all the way
to Rivière des Prairies.

The name Pie-IX always makes me think of the first Vatican
Council of 1870-71, and the promulgation of the dogma of
Papal Infallibility. It isn't very long since the tone of Catholi-
cism in the city was much in the spirit of the lamented Pius the
Ninth. What he would have said about contemporary Montréal
church architecture, or about *aggiornamento* or the opening to
the left, or Vatican Two, confounds me as I think of it. I don't
believe anyone would name a *ruelle*, let alone a six-lane main
artery, after Pius the Ninth, at this time. John, yes: Pius, no.
Things are moving fast.

We cross the bridge fast because it has only two lanes and
there's always a press of traffic behind, the river wide and black
and very cold beneath. Swing to the right, right again along the
north shore to Saint-Vincent de Paul, left here, stop at the grocery store for a dozen Black Horse which will be drunk in the
dressing room after the game, win or lose, and on to the edge of
town to the Centre Sportif where, according to local legend,
the Rocket and some of his life-long friends have played pickup
hockey on Sunday afternoons since he retired five years ago. He
still has his shot, they say around the arena, and from the blueline in, his legs.

The arena is shaped in what seems to my ungeometrical eye
to be the arc of a parabola described by beautifully curving,
powerful steel beams covered by crimped steel roofing and ter-
minated by brick walls. It's about the size of a dirigible hangar
and is surely the most useful building in the community,
churches and schools apart. There's a parking lot at the main
entrance, accommodating maybe fifty cars, and just past the
building a flat expanse of ground which might be a soccer or

football field. I've never seen it in daylight. Away off to your right, a very dim shape in this darkest week of the year, looms a building of unmistakably institutional shape, a college or an orphanage, evidently not a convent school because of the heavy predominance of males in the neighbourhood. Its presence probably explains those lurking grey-headed Christian Brothers with their collars like divided spades, who pace in the runway around the ice-surface at all times, keeping an eye on their students' development.

'Il a quitté son aile, l'idiot.'

'Jeu de position là-bas. Position!'

Strictly speaking, this is the Laval Community Arena, but since Laval is so expansive and sprawling a collection of suburbs, I prefer to associate it with the small township where it lies, named for a Saint of very charitable reputation.

LIGUE DES FRANCS COPAINS

	W	L	T	P
GARS:	5	1	2	12
CHUMS:	3	3	2	8
AMIS:	2	2	4	8
COPAINS:	1	5	2	4

I'm sorry but amused to note that the Guys, the Chums, and the Pals are still beating hell out of the Comrades. I'd have preferred it otherwise – this is a local French league, much like ours, but on a grander scale. They play a devastatingly good brand of hockey and have no prohibition on board checking and other impolitenesses. One time a couple of seasons back, a disgruntled forward in their league, objecting to a bad call, struck the referee – his close friend – in the eye with his stick. He got carried away, I suppose, and so in another sense did the official, who lost the sight of the eye permanently. *Les francs copains.* There's a big sign hanging inside the main entrance giving the current standings in their league, the Comrades securely in the cellar. In the foyer are hung dozens of photographs: the blessing and opening of the arena fifteen years ago, this year's local Junior-B team, a championship Pee-Wee team ranked behind an enormous trophy as tall as anyone on the club, the Rocket in a referee's striped shirt kneeling in the middle of a crowd of autograph-seekers.

There are arenas like this all over Montréal and the suburbs, with a foyer much used for ping-pong, for meeting your girl friend, for loitering. In this one anyway I've never seen any rough stuff, no rowdyism, no delinquents. Often a lad of thirteen will hold the door open for you, if you're carrying kitbag, sticks, skates. Plenty of long hair, and some remarkably chic girls of twelve or thirteen, but nothing even close to criminal.

We pass one of the gangways as we go to the dressing room. Two Pee-Wee teams are on the ice, working out at either end. Their hour, six-thirty to seven-thirty, seems to be devoted to shooting and play-making practice, not to league games which are likely played through the week or on Sunday afternoon. The players don't look at all like little boys dressed in outsized equipment. They look like hockey players, having played the game for seven or eight years, since they could stand up on skates. They have moves that I, who never played the game seriously growing up in Toronto, will never acquire: they shoot better than I do, feed a pass better, head-man the puck. They have the game in their legs and arms and hearts from the cradle.

Waiting for our league prexy to unlock the dressing rooms, I watch what the kids are doing. Tonight they're working on faking the goalie out, a line of forwards at the blueline carrying the puck in, one after the other, with a spindly defenceman rapping it out to the next man after the goalie has moved on the play. They don't shoot from the blueline on this exercise, but skate in close, perhaps take a head fake or a stick fake, move to the right or left to persuade the goalie to commit himself, so they can swing with the puck and shoot behind him as he goes the wrong way. At the west end of the rink, the team is dressed in green, apple-green sweaters with yellow trim, which makes me think of the church we passed coming out, a broad band of yellow around the midsection, and pants in a darker green; most wear headgear. Two defencemen, not taking shooting drill, are skating backwards from side to side of the ice, practising passing the puck forward while moving back, necessary for a defenceman and not as easy as it looks when done right.

Groaning behind me. Carpenter. The dressing rooms must be open now, time to dress so as to be on the ice the moment it's been reflooded at seven-thirty. We only have an hour's ice-time this year, but hope for an hour and a half next season.

Carpenter was taking a drink as I came past, filling himself with ice-cold water, glugging, not a good idea before the game. He straightened.

'Sixty minutes tonight, kid?'

'Sure,' I said, 'I'm in shape, Fred.' I shouldn't have said that. He looked ashen. He could have been a good player too, lots better than me. He said, 'I play, vomit, play. You know.'

'No, you don't. Not in this league.' We went on down to dressing room four to get ready. Paul Bowsfield had a dozen sticks he'd picked up in a job lot, good ones, and some of us took a look at them. Brian Tansey, an insurance man of twenty-nine, our best defenceman, who more or less keeps an eye on Carpenter, had a small dig for me.

'You were using a number seven last week.'

'So what? I'm getting the puck into the air.'

'Yeah, but you're missing passes, and the puck keeps hopping over your stick, damn you. Try a five.'

He had a point. I bought two fives from Bowsfield, cost me four bucks, and I didn't notice any improvement. I missed passes just the same.

In this city hockey is the chief social cement. The Sportsman's League plays pretty poor hockey because most of us are in there once a week for fun. But there are five or six really good players, all of whom play in other, better leagues. Seymour plays in the Town of Mount Royal Senior. One week he was complaining to me about the play there.

'I'm getting beat where I shouldn't get beat. There's this guy Gary Paxton, he had three goals on me last night.'

'Yeah?'

'He's pretty good. He played a couple seasons out west.'

That got my ear. 'Where out west?'

'In the Western League. Where else?'

I thought somebody might be kidding somebody, because the WHL is a very fast minor league, full of guys like Charlie Burns who had three seasons with the Bruins, or Andy

Hebenton who holds the N H L ironman record, around seven hundred consecutive games with New York and Boston. One season he had over thirty goals, which means that at that time he was one of the best hockey players alive. So if Paxton played in the W H L he was bound to be damned good. When I got home that night I checked him out in the record book (I have record books going back a good long way) and there he was: PAXTON, GARY. Born 1940, and the rest, and he really did play for Los Angeles, 1963-64, 1964-65, and he had fifteen goals last year, which means that he wasn't just hanging on.

He probably realized that he was twenty-five and about at his peak. If you haven't made it at least to the American League by then, you likely won't ever make it to the N H L. I suppose he figured he'd gone about as far as he could and decided to come back to Montréal to settle into some kind of career, playing amateur hockey on the side. This happens in all sports; the phenomenon is familiar in sandlot baseball. You go out to throw the ball around and some guy is cruising back of second in that unmistakable way. Or get up a weekly game of touch football among friends in a park, and one fine summer Saturday somebody shows up who suddenly fires the ball seventy yards with a nice easy arm motion, and it turns out that he played for N D G and had a tryout with the Alouettes, that he might have had a football scholarship to Arizona State but chose to stay home and look after his mother.

Seymour could have signed with the Rangers' organization when he was seventeen, but his parents didn't want him to turn into a hockey bum. 'If they'd only known how I'd turn out,' he says, 'they'd have signed, they'd have signed.'

'My son, the painter,' I say, and we laugh. But he keeps wondering how things would have worked out if he'd turned pro. I tell him he'd never have made it; they had Worsley and Marcel Paillé, and some other guys, but he keeps wondering.

'You're better off where you are.'

'Yeah, but I'm not playing well. It's the quality of the competition.'

He's quite right. Playing behind me isn't doing him any good. He gets a lot of shots but all from the wrong places, because I'm not good enough to jockey the forwards over to where they should be. Still, I'm playing with Seymour who was wanted by the Ranger chain, and he's playing with Gary Paxton who had fifteen goals in the WHL last year, see what I mean? And Paxton was playing with Hebenton and Burns who once upon a time played with Andy Bathgate and Johnny Bucyk. I feel as though I belonged to the club in a small way, and it's relations like these that give society its meaning. Me and Andy!

There's a dining and conversation group in the city called the Veterans. *Not* an ex-service club, which can be awfully tedious, but a collection of types who have been associated with hockey as player or coach or even as owner. Every year they give a big dinner with speakers, newspaper coverage, and awards. Elmer Ferguson always comes, and gives the function a fine advance write-up; they tape some of the speeches for the sports shows. This year their big award went to Claude Provost who beat out Gordie Howe for first all-star last season; everybody was there. Newsy Lalonde was there, who used to live a block away from me back of Maplewood. King Clancy was there, sitting with a lot of hockey men from Ottawa. Hooley Smith is dead now, but some of the old Maroons got to the dinner, Jimmy Ward, whose son has made it in major-league ball. Men like these have associations going back before 1910, the Arenas, the Wanderers, the Silver Seven, Montréal AAA.

In the Forum Tavern after the game, talking to Léon the waiter, we ask him to tell us who is the greatest player he ever saw, and he tells us the story of the time Maurice scored five.

'Gordie Howe is a better hockey player,' he says generously 'and Bill looked better than anybody. But the Rocket ... there was never anybody like him. There *will* never be anybody like him. One time the Rangers hired this boxer, this heavyweight, Dill. The Rocket flattened him with one punch. If it hadn't been for injuries, he could have played three or four more seasons.'

'He cut a tendon,' somebody says, 'and he was putting on weight. They were calling him *pépère.*'

'He's still playing. He plays every Sunday out in Saint-Vincent. They say he can still score.'

'Sure he can score.'

'He could score,' says Léon, 'on the Devil himself. If Maurice was dying and the goalie gave him the angle, he'd get up and score. I saw him carry Earl Seibert in from the blueline on his shoulders and score with one hand. I saw him....'

He goes off for more beer talking happily to himself.

Before our game Fred Carpenter was babbling loosely and happily about a set of irons he'd picked up, a steal. I didn't follow what he said because I was concentrating on dressing and taping my sticks, and thinking about the game, wondering which line I'd be on against, Leo's line or Kenny, Eric, and Eddie? A lot of the quality of your play depends on your checks. I'd sooner be on against Leo's line because the forward coming in against me will be either Pierre or Chaloub, depending on how we line up and which side I'm playing. I turn best to the right and should play on that side, but as we often have somebody missing we shuffle our alignment every time out.

Playing against their other line, I'm too slow. All I can do is try to jam the wing on the boards, while avoiding the appearance of sin. Tactics, tactics and rituals; hockey isn't a game but a complex set of rituals. That night Carpenter violated them all. He wandered up and down, smoking, which you never do before a game, and he was talking too much, in a disconnected way. Once or twice I saw Paul Bowsfield, who more or less captains our side, give him a strange evaluating look. Seymour seemed upset about something too.

The silent lines of communication that develop in a dressing room before a game are subtle, tight, and unsmiling. They don't vary. Years ago some individual pencilled the single word 'Boisvert' over the hook where I hang my clothes. Boisvert, if that was his name, may long ago have died or moved away, but nobody will remove the name, and that's simply where I sit, facing Seymour. Tommy sits on my left by the door to the showers and George sits next to Seymour facing me. George and I take turns bringing the beer, twelve cans, one for each player and one over for the man who brings it. Watch how the Leafs come on the ice behind Johnny Bower. Shack is always the first man out. When the Canadiens take their warmup, Terry Harper is almost always the last man to go off. At the start of the game, you skate back and say something to the goalie, whacking his pads. After the game, if you've won, you meet the goalie coming to the bench and congratulate him, whether he had a good game and kept you in there or was just lucky, or even if he was lousy and you had to outscore the other team eight to seven. You just do this.

When Carpenter kept on horsing around, getting up, sitting down, smoking, getting in people's way, he was violating many silent agreements.

That night I was first out of the dressing room as usual. When I'd been on the ice, which was very fast, fresh, and new, for a couple of minutes, the others came on, we took the goalie's warm-up and then Paul gave us the line-up for the night and the game started. We only had three defencemen out. Polsky hadn't turned out, so the arrangement was that Tansey and Carpenter would start and I would spell them off alternately; each of us would get some short shifts and some doubles. Brian was playing a strong rushing game, as he always does, and we kept the puck in their end for the first minutes. Soon Carpenter hollered, and I hopped over the boards and took him off, and things were all right for another three minutes.

Then the roof fell in. Brian had played around six or seven minutes, which he can do because he skates strongly and knows how to pace himself. But when Carpenter came on with me, and I had to change over to the left side where I'm uncomfortable, we gave up three goals, bang, bang, bang, with the game still young. The first was my fault. I got beat on the play but good and told Seymour so, as he fished the puck out of the net. But on the second I was nowhere near the play, and I was glad, because Seymour was pretty red-faced over it. After the goal he said something to Carpenter which was evidently fairly blunt. It was a funny play – the last thing I saw was somebody's glove deflecting the flying puck. The third goal was a clean play, a two-on-one situation where I had to play the puck carrier or anticipate a pass, and I made a wrong guess.

When you get down three in the early part of a game, two things can happen. Either you play stronger, hold them, and come on when they tire towards the end, or you fall apart, lose your cohesion, and stop skating. This night we fell apart. Oh, we got one goal to bring it up to three to one, and it looked for a second as if we might pick up, then they got it right back and led at the end of the first period, four to one. We only have ice-time for two periods, and the second was worse than the first. Nothing rolled right for us, the forwards weren't skating, and they weren't coming back. I took to falling all over the place out of haste and lack of confidence. Midway through the second period, Carpenter went off and could be heard some distance back of the bench vomiting into a fountain. We got bombed, seven to one. Trooping into the dressing room after the game, we saw the clogged fountain loaded with expelled matter; it was a dismal sight, but appropriate.

Silence, oh, boy, like you could spread it on pumpernickel, thick, heavy. I put the dozen Black Horse in the middle of the floor, and nobody dived for it, very unusual, that. Finally I popped it open, took one myself, handed out a few. Somebody took off a jersey; somebody fiddled with his skates. Tommy looked soberly at a cracked stick.

You could hear singing from the next dressing room.

After a couple of minutes of this Seymour rose and addressed the meeting: 'I don't mind losing,' he started off, gathering steam as he proceeded. 'I think I can say that. I've lost a lot of games in my time. I've had my off nights, but this wasn't one of them, and I don't want to lose any more like that one. If there are guys here who don't care enough about the league to turn up sober – I'm not naming any names and I'm not talking about any one person – I don't want to play behind them. It's dangerous. You can get hurt on a goal-post or in the corners, playing like that, and you can injure somebody else perma-nently, and you might just as well take the game and hand it to the other team. A beer in the dressing room afterwards, that's fine, everybody likes that, but nobody but a fool, and I mean a fool, drinks before the game. That's all.' He sat down and started taking off his pads.

Carpenter looked up from his skates – he'd had his head down while Seymour was talking – and said briefly, 'I quit.' He got the rest of his things off, didn't bother about a shower, and went out, shutting the door quietly.

Bowsfield said, 'I was going to talk to him about it.'

'Does anybody think I'm wrong?' Seymour said. 'He could hurt any of us. He put their second goal in the net himself, just batted it in with his glove. I suppose he was trying to clear it, but what the hell, a goalie has no protection against that.'

'He'll be back,' somebody said.

'I think he'll be back,' I said.

'Sure, after Christmas.' We have to take a break at Christmas. 'Did he come up with you, Brian?'

'Naw, not tonight; he got away from the office early. I think he caught a ride with Yvan.'

'Does he drink in the office?'

'Not in the office, no. Right after.'

'I didn't think he looked so bad,' I said.

'You could smell it.'

'Ah.'

I collected quarters from the few who had taken a beer, picked up the remaining cans and my equipment and hustled out to stick them in the car. Carpenter was standing at the coffee counter under the Ligue des Francs Copains sign. I joined him; he looked bereft.

'See you after New Year's,' I said cheerfully.

He said nothing, just drank his coffee, shivered, and went outside. I don't know who drove him home; he certainly didn't come with us. After he left there was the usual kidding around at the coffee counter.

'Tonight you couldn't make a wrong move,' Seymour said jovially to Leo, 'the way you hang around that red line.'

Leo grinned at me. 'You want to play with more confidence,' he said. 'Try charging the forwards. I don't mean so as to hurt anybody.'

There were exchanges of holiday greetings, kind of a line-up in which we all shook hands and wished each other a good Christmas. Tansey looked around, wondering where Carpenter was.

'He's gone,' Seymour said glumly. 'I didn't catch him. I meant to.'

'After Christmas,' I said.

'That's it.'

When we went out to the cars, it had stopped snowing; there

were solid wet cakes of white on every car, oozing water down windows. It was growing colder. The sky had cleared, and you could see the clouds moving and the stars back of them. Car doors slammed. People joked about the lopsided score, gradually the parking lot cleared. When Seymour had had his weekly argument with the league president about who should transship his equipment to the Town of Mount Royal Arena, we drove away.

'Ron is taking care of it?'

'What?'

'Your pads.'

'Oh, that.' He lit a cigar Ron had given him, and a rich vapour filled the car. I coughed critically. 'That's all right, now,' said Seymour, 'this is a good cigar. I wish I had Ron's dough.'

'You will when you're dead.'

'I suppose so.' We drove in silence through Saint-Vincent to the highway, through the underpass, up the ramp, onto the approach to the bridge. Coming back into town, the approach slopes sharply down and there is a fine view of the river and the lights along the dark shore. You almost seem to swoop down like a plane, and the lights of the town rush to meet you and the dark water somehow draws your eyes. You have to take care, coming off the bridge, as the traffic divides into streams headed for various suburbs across the northern part of the city.

Tonight, perhaps because of the snow, there was much bright reflection from the river, white on dark, with faint moving pin-pricks of red and green here and there. I felt cold, and the cigar smoke was oppressive. Down Pie-IX in the centre lane southbound, we were bowling along pretty good, catching the lights in sequence, heading for the Metropolitan West, and a few beers and some sandwiches in a tavern on the Main called Le Gobelet, where we always go. By the time we were across town, the cold had become intense and we were glad to get out of the car and into the clatter and warmth of Le Gobelet where we sat watching colour TV, going over the game, eating till it was time to go home.

Three weeks later the shoe was on the other foot; we got off to a grand start, got the right roll from the puck every time. I played my first decent game of the season and the rest of the club was hustling too. We won it, three to one, which started us off on a winning streak that lasted quite a time.

Tansey, Polsky, and I played defence; the other fellow never came back, although we hear of him sometimes through Brian. Once, after a game we won really big, Seymour and I stood around the foyer for a while watching the kids come and go around the ping-pong tables. Just by the entrance there's a little door which might lead to the building superintendent's office, and over it stands a big grey plaster statue of the Blessed Virgin with the Child in her arms; the statue has a circular electric halo. It all fits in.

Seymour took me by the arm for a second. 'We have a lot in common, you know.'

I agreed with him silently.

He said, 'We take a pretty high moral line, don't we?'

I said I thought we did.

'You know,' he said slowly, 'if the position has a defect – I'm not sure it has – it would be self-righteousness, wouldn't it?'

I thought he was right, and said so.

Light Shining out of Darkness

SOUTH OF BOULEVARD MONT-ROYAL as far as Rachel, from the Main eastwards past Papineau, lies the country of the *ruelles*. Close to the Main are streets like Henri-Julien, de Bullion, Hôtel de Ville, one-way north or south, which in another place might be considered slums; not in Montréal. Going east past Christophe-Colomb towards de Lanaudière, Fabre, past des Erables and Parthenais, you discover small enclaves which are clearly the homes of comfortable older citizens; the grocery stores grow imperceptibly more prosperous in appearance, their paint is fresher.

Ah, but Henri-Julien, Drôlet, that's the real thing. Hundreds of young families with three or four children, the youngest a bare-bottomed infant creeping along the *ruelle* curb, already trained to evade the creeping delivery vans which sometimes bump along the pitted track, while his sister, maybe four, in a smudged undershirt, eyes him as he learns his way....

They are narrow blocks, buildings fronting on parallel main streets and backing on a shared alley. Each long block is made vertebrate by the crawling teeming *ruelle* life, traced out in the shape of an H, or a pair of goalposts, with a very long crossbar running up the middle of the block and two short uprights at the ends.

When these streets were laid out, before the turn of the century, there was no automobile traffic, and there are no private driveways in the district. The houses, and the enormous stately multi-family dwellings, not precisely apartment buildings, crowd against each other. Back of them are the alleys which once upon a time must have been long networks of stables. They aren't a convenient width for automobile traffic, though you can get a car in or out. Trying to ease into a former stable, you have to scramble around a very sharp right angle as you aim for the door. It's tricky in snow.

On the lesser thoroughfares, the houses will be painted brick, doorways flush with the sidewalk, three storeys high, and very often they will have ornamental cornices in wood painted light green, pale blue, most frequently pink. Atop these cornices there will be two or three little minarets or globes or vanes, all in woodwork. When you examine them closely, they are evidently not the work of master craftsmen who worked in extreme detail; there are no intricate carvings, no highly developed skill. They are the work of adze and plane, executed roughly, the same shapes repeated hundreds of times all through the neighbourhood, but never too close together. From the sidewalk there is an impression of delightful variety, heightened by the colours of successive thick coats of paint.

You enter the house directly from the sidewalk, there being neither areaway nor front garden, nor is there space between houses. The windows have snow shutters, again executed in rough but useful carpentry. In the poorer parts of the district, the shutters are sometimes missing, the windows inadequately boarded over and the house left empty. But mostly these places present a rich family life which, having no outlet in front but the sidewalk, tends to proliferate in the alley, safer for the abundance of babies. Sometimes back there you'll find a small, balding, grass plot with ten adults roosting on it and God knows how many kids hollering ... toy trucks with a wheel gone, orange plastic Really-Ride-'Em tractors.

The main streets east and west are (from the north) Marie-Anne, Rachel, and Duluth, and a slow summer bicycle ride east along any of them will display the variety of customs and of wealth. Go along Marie-Anne and your way east from the Main is at first narrow and crowded, the business in the small grocery stores done half in the street. Motorists are circumspect. Men load meat in trucks from some wholesale *salaison*. The slope of the street decreases as you come towards Saint-Denis, the pavement widens. If you were to ride as far as Fabre, you would spot on the southeast corner a line of half a dozen row houses which could have been built yesterday, they shine so with fresh paint and gleaming woodwork, and they aren't restored town houses for television executives either, though each has a television aerial. They are two storeys high, and the curtains have all been starched this morning.

North and south are some big important streets like Saint-Hubert, and here again you'll find a kind of dwelling that is

perhaps indigenous. I mean those long rows of tall broad unin-
terrupted buildings that can't be called apartment buildings
because the units are not connected by interior corridors, nor,
very often, by heating lines. These huge piles are approached by
outside staircases – the beautiful Montréal staircases – front and
rear, so that you don't enter the building and traverse a hall to
reach your front door. You climb an outside staircase and enter
an independent dwelling, often totally separated from the rest
of the building except by the plumbing. You will heat your
home at your own expense with one or another of those space
heaters which each winter effect multiple accidental fires and
smotherings. There is something very *montréalais* about such
buildings, which combine independence with strength and
bulk. Yet the staircases are often of an extraordinarily pleasing
lightness and apparent fragility, front and back. Take a look at
Le Montagnard which fronts on Saint-Hubert and backs on ...
well it ought to back on an alley but actually backs on Avénue
de Chateaubriand, which makes me think of rich bloody steaks,
of Atala and René, and of the gypsies in Canada. ...

Shvetz and I were sitting in the Gérard Marcil Tavern, corner
Saint-Hubert and Duluth, REPAS COMPLETS, waiting for
Lazarovich, in from Ottawa for a weekend. He wanted to talk
to the Old Man, whom we could see plainly sitting across the
room, but whom we didn't want to join till Lazarovich came, as
he's the contact.

This tavern may have been successively a *caisse populaire*, a
grocery store, and a small warehouse for novelties and sundries
before becoming a tavern. It's the corner property in a big
building, a true apartment building, this one, painted in a matte
shadowy silver colour over what might be compressed gypsum
siding, a very cosy spot on an iron-cold deep February night.
We had come there at Lazarovich's command, an hour before,
so that he could combine an evening with us and a chat with the
Old Man, Petroff, the patriarch of Montréal gypsies. Afterwards we would go around the corner and up de Chateaubri-
and, if we didn't miss it in the darkness, to see Tom. The cold
held on hard, but the tavern entrances were screened by inner
winter doors, and we were sitting at the back of the room.

Shvetz said, a bit restively, 'He knows everything.'

'Petroff?'

'He's been everywhere. We'll see if we can get him to talk.'

About ten o'clock Lazarovich arrived in a rush. He's always in a rush on these flying trips; he may find the pace a little slow in Ottawa. He came to the table and said without ceremony, as though we'd seen him the day before, 'Let's move.'

We picked up our ten glasses and followed him across to the table where the Old Man was sitting, his beard fluffed out down the front of his overcoat to the third button, his bright large deep-set eyes looking slowly around the room like distant early warning radars, maintaining order by a searching glare, anticipating disaster.

'How are you, Mr Petroff?' said Lazarovich. He sat down, and after a moment we did too.

'I'm an Old Man,' said Petroff; you could hear the capital letters.

'He always says that,' said Lazarovich aside.

'Could we buy you some beer?'

'One or two, I think, no more. I'm an Old Man and I don't need as much as I did in the old times. This is good beer,' he said generously. 'I've always liked the Canadian beer, not like some. In Hungary, we find a native beer which is light but drinkable, but there, of course, there is much else to drink, and in the Ukraine, and among the Slovenes. The Slovenes are always quarrelling with one another, naturally, and haven't much time for drink, so the gypsies consume the excess.' He laughed, took up a full glass and swallowed it. 'These glasses are too small.'

'I haven't seen you for a while,' said Lazarovich, 'not since my party when Vanya was born. Do you remember?'

'Very well. That was the last time I danced. I danced with your wife, and with Tom's.' He stared hard at Shvetz. 'You were there, with your jokes. You were very happy.'

'I've given up joking,' said Shvetz, 'I've become a family man. I have responsibilities.'

'That happens to all you young men. Look at me, now, I'm seventy-eight and have buried three wives, two in Europe, one in America, and I have no responsibilities except my position. I used to move around, a year in Sofia, a year on the road. Even after I came here I was moving all the time. I was with carnivals, with a Wheel of Fortune, then the Nifty Girlie Show, then with the Bingo, "*Jouez-au-Bingo, sieurs et dames. Venez, venez, dix sous seulement, ça commence encore, ça roule tout en ronde.*" I am never settled down.' He gave Shvetz a hard stare. 'What responsibilities have you?'

'Well, I'm learning the clarinet, I....'

'You have settled down to learn the clarinet. Good. You will be a master, since you take it so seriously, but you will not travel, play in a village orchestra, for your dinner and a bed. You will never accompany a dancing bear. For a dancing bear one needs a small drum, about the size of the larger tambourine.'

'Tambourine means "little drum",' said Lazarovich.

'Not at all the same; it is a mistake in the name. A tambourine is struck with the open palm, and has no base, no resonator. There are metal plates let into the side, which vibrate as the head is struck. There are different sizes.'

'It's strictly a percussion instrument,' said Shvetz

'Not at all, not at all. If you have different sizes you can simulate chords, and you can vary the beat – there's much music in the tambourine. But you are right in this respect, that a single tambourine is a percussion instrument, not more.'

'For a dancing bear.'

'No,' said Petroff wearily, 'not for a dancing bear.'

'What then?'

'For a dancing bear,' he began again, 'a small drum is best, with a boy to play the bagpipe. You interrupted me. But in this country you do not have that sort of village entertainment. You will never go from village to village in that way, as I did for forty years. It is a kind of freedom you cannot hope to know.'

Shvetz prides himself on being a free soul, and he began to protest. 'There are other ways. I gig around. There are dates.'

'Have you played Mascouche? Saint-Jovite? Amqui?'

'Well, no.'

'I have.'

They began a discussion of freedom and responsibility which was beyond me, my mind being too heavy and concrete for any flight of abstruse reasoning. I sat on, following the talk at some distance, sometimes getting ten cents' worth of pistachio nuts in a paper cone to go with my beer. After an hour's debate, Lazarovich went to the bathroom, and from there to call Tom, to see if we should come by.

'You must see him,' said Mr Petroff, 'see him, he is a fine young man who will replace me when I die. He has a wife and three daughters but he is free … free. He will not remain where he is.'

Lazarovich came back from the phone. 'It's all right,' he said, 'he's in. It's only a minute from here.'

'I hope so,' said Shvetz, clearly disgruntled. 'It's bloody cold.'

The Old Man began to laugh. 'Dance, dance, that will warm you.' As we went to the door, he lifted his hand in a grave salute. We went out into black cold.

If you blink you'll miss Avenue de Chateaubriand. In this part of town, it is really an alley with pretensions, too narrow for cars to pass. It starts at Roy and runs north just past Marie-Anne where it is interrupted by the railroad right-of-way, the iron curtain of Montréal which severs the life flow of all the streets in the east end except the biggest, as far out as D'Iberville. North of the tracks it begins again somewhere back of de Fleurimont, running into the north end where it gradually becomes a real street.

Where Tom lives you can't park. To do so, you would have to climb right up on the sidewalk, and at that it would be hard for somebody else to get past. Sometimes at the north end of this block an undertaker parks a hearse for several hours, and then the street is effectively closed off. As in an alley, the big buildings fronting on the next main street present their backs to the passer-by. Tom lives in what must be the back part of Le Montagnard or one of its neighbours on Saint-Hubert: but for him the entrance is on de Chateaubriand. The approach to his third-floor quarters is embellished by a really beautiful spiral staircase with a delicate iron rail rising in a graceful curve. I don't deny the staircase is dangerous in winter, when you can't put your bare hand on the railing, and when you have to watch your footing very carefully.

As we ascended Lazarovich said, 'A man fell down here one

night straight to the bottom. He was a Hungarian, may have been drunk. Killed instantly.' It was hellishly dark climbing, but as we came to the second floor, a blind shot up on the door to your left and bright light streamed out; a pair of female eyes glared angrily at us. Then suddenly the blind descended and it was as dark as before. On the third-floor platform, right at the top, you're apt to feel slightly dizzy if you look down at the black rectangle below, whose centre, an oblong grass plot, is ringed by upwards-pointing metal spikes. There is the impression of an elevator shaft of indefinite length, without entry except from above.

It was very dark on the balcony. All at once a door flew open and we were flooded and surrounded by intensely bright light. Tom stood in the doorway, beckoning us in. Lazarovich went first, then Shvetz, then me. While introductions were circulating, I stood blinking and looking around, a little confused by the wave of light and colour. I had a rich, mixed, impression of much pale electric light in which were splashed patch after patch of brilliant colour, high up in the room. I scarcely understood the introductions except to get the sense that I was meeting Tom and his wife, old friends of Lazarovich.

As my eyes grew accustomed to the light, I saw that all over the room, mounted on dully shining polished wooden stands, on top of the taller articles of furniture, stood a great fleet of what seemed at first to be children's toy sailboats. Examining them more closely, I could see that far from being playthings they were immensely delicate and detailed works of art, models of famous sailing vessels of the sixteenth and seventeenth centuries. Their sails, sometimes pale waxen yellow like old parchment, sometimes closer to an oily transparent brown, sometimes nearly white canvas stippled with almost invisible brown dots, were emblazoned with royal and naval arms, purple and red and blue and gold, gleaming richly in thick oil laid on the heavy fabric of the sails. The decks of these ships were hand-worked in strips of miniature planking fastened with nails so small as almost to disappear. Hulls were varnished in hard thick transparent coats, and sometimes the keels were coated in sheets of shining copper, polished and giving back an image of one's amazed inspection.

This was a fantastic dream of vanished fleets, Drake's *Revenge*, galleons of the Armada, Admiral Blake's flagship in his Dutch wars, Hudson's *Half Moon*, ship after ship, all famous, all worked with magnificent accuracy, all in splendid and royal colours. As I stood there saucer-eyed, taking this impression in, the others began to laugh softly at my amazement and talk began, and a potent fruit punch was served.

Sometimes a calm scene like this, a rounded period in the life of the imagination, will rest in one's faculties, stay, rotate, restate itself over and over in changing colours and meanings, exciting feelings, instincts, memory, imagination, seeming to have special powers to enlighten and give form to the rest of our lives. Standing there in the queer narrow living room, almost a scarcely enclosed balcony projecting over nothing, a bit drafty, a bit poor in its other furnishings, I was mysteriously overwhelmed by this various and splendid sight with feelings of a hidden and immense joy. I was smiling and transfixed, and the remembrance of the sight long after retains the capacity to direct and strengthen all my ways of feeling, so that the life of de Chateaubriand mixes itself irrecoverably with my suspicions of the possibility of goodness, of the memorable life.

Confusedly smiling and wondering, I felt grateful when Tom's wife put a glass of rosy punch in my hand. I drank it at once, and immediately began to feel sleepy. I found a seat beside her – I never learned her name – and began to look at her admiringly. She had small dark features, beautifully composed, giving her an exotic loveliness; she looked like an elf; she looked like the gypsy she was. As my eyes moved from her around the room and back, she laughed soundlessly.

'My husband is in the Marine Museum,' she said, 'and these are his work. He has a great collection, you know, one of the best in the world, all his.'

I said thoughtfully that such work must require great powers of concentration and great skill.

'They've been written up and photographed. There was a big story in colour on them in *Weekend Magazine*.'

I remembered having seen the story, but when I said so she was not impressed. 'He could do this work anywhere, for the Royal Navy, for the Institute of Naval History, but these are his, and even so this is not his life work.'

'What does he do?'

'Why, he leads us. Listen.'

Tom was discussing Romany history, of which he was certain a learned exponent. 'The aboriginal home of the Tzigany or Romany folk, or as they are called in English the Gypsies, is shrouded in the obscurity of prehistory. Their English name ascribes to them an Egyptian origin, but this is certainly false. Their language – our language – is structurally of immense antiquity, being closest in its morphologies to Sanskrit, closer than any modern tongue except perhaps Lithuanian. From those primitive vocabularies we possess (unfortunately much mixed with loan-words), it is possible to hypothesize a location in Northwestern India. From there we made our way overland, south of the Aral and through Persia, appearing in recorded European history in early Christian times. We have always been travellers, free, moving.' He broke off.

His wife said proudly, 'Tom is preparing the first scientific lexicon of Romany.'

'For English use?'

'Of course.' She and Lazarovich and Shvetz began to talk to Tom about his chances of publication, of an offer from a great university press, and of some of his appearances on television. It seemed that he had done much, worked very hard for a long time, to redress some of his people's legal and political disabilities connected with citizenship, conscription, and taxation. I grew very drowsy. Once his wife said to me confidentially, 'He's been interviewed on TV twice.'

'I know,' I said hazily, getting up to go to the toilet at the end of an extraordinarily narrow hall. As I poked my way past an undersized space-heater, past baby-carriages and playpens, three little girls popped successively out of three doorways. They were exactly like their mother. She followed me, glass in hand, and knelt among them, fondling them and crooning to them. Their appearance so late at night in this tiny isolated apartment intensified my earlier feelings of wonder. They smiled and began to sing sweetly to their mother, an old song in the minor about the larks in wintertime.

In the living room, a technical philological discussion had

now begun. I drank off my punch, accepted a refill with misgivings, went to the bathroom, and got back in time for Lazarovich's reluctant good-night. 'I'm only in town for a day and a night,' he said.

They stood, black silhouettes, in the doorway, warning us of the steps. I saw them framed in the brilliance of their room as we went back down.

'What's his last name?' I asked Lazarovich.

He paused at the bottom of the spiral. 'It's very funny, you know that? I've known him for years. I can't tell you his last name.'

Avenue de Chateaubriand grows deadly cold after midnight in February. We moved off, and parted at the corner. Much later in the year, coming back alone and unannounced to drop in on Tom and his wife, I discovered to my sorrow that they had moved on.

Bicultural Angela

NOT SO LONG AGO, in her mid-teens, growing up in Stover-
ville seventy miles from the Québec border, Angela Mary
Robinson heard her mother exclaim to a visitor from Montréal,
'I do so much want to know what is happening to you people.
So exciting, everything one hears about the new Québec.'
   Angela had not heard her mother express this view before.
'Is Westmount burning?' said Mrs. Robinson playfully.
   The visitor, an elegant bond salesman spending a weekend
on somebody's houseboat, raised an eyebrow with a polite air
of one who has heard the tune before. 'Do you really want to
know?' he said.
   'I think it is my duty.'
   'Why not subscribe to *Le Devoir*? They cover the province so
fully that they hardly talk about anything else. It would cost you
twenty dollars a year, but it's worth much more.'
   Mrs. Robinson sighed. 'Ah, but you see, I don't read a word
of French.'
   Thinking this over afterwards, Angela decided that her
mother's words implied several things: hypocrisy, frivolity,
obstinate persistence in a dangerous prejudice. She was old
enough to spot the tone in her mother's voice which meant that
Mrs. Robinson was attempting to please by pretending an
interest in an obscure, probably trivial, special subject.
   Rejecting Queen's and the Conservatory, Angela went to
Trinity College in the University of Toronto and wore pastel
sweaters from Holt-Renfrew, oatmeal-tweed skirts and a single
strand of pearls through freshman and sophomore years. After
that, involved with the production of a fugitive film and learning French voraciously, she switched to coarsely knit Italian
sweaters in bright reds and yellows fitting loosely around the
hips. She discarded skirts for slacks, often rather tight. She had
a smart, navy-blue duffle coat. In her last year, she subscribed to
the international edition of *Le Monde* and acquired a startling
expertise connected with the General Agreement on Tariffs and
Trade.

She read the film quarterlies, having been deeply influenced by Marshall McLuhan, and had a vague notion of doing a master's degree on one of the media. By graduation, Angela Mary knew definitely that the one place to be, in Canada in the mid-sixties, was French Montréal, not Westmount, which she knew well from weekends, nor the McGill campus, but *le vrai Montréal*, as she considered it, of the Bonsecours market, old picturesque restored Montréal. She also had the idea that there was a lot of activity at the Office National du Film and Radio-Canada, and she went to a lot of trouble to get herself a job in CBC-Montréal. Not much of a job. She was a trainee programme organizer in FM, and hoped that she might have a chance to get into French-language programming if she worked very hard on her spoken French and cultivated obvious French types around the studios.

She took to spending a lot of time in various Montréal cafés and bars. When her duties took her as far south as the main building on Dorchester West, she would spend an hour after the completion of her errand at that little place just west of Mackay where you never knew whom you might run into. She watched the French girls, the way they did their hair, their make-up, and began to experiment with her looks, with metallic green eyeshadow, at first very discreetly applied. She bought some hairpieces and began to tease the acquired hair and her own into extremely bouffant situations. Whether in this she was fully *dans le vent* remains an open question. She discarded slacks for dresses like Petula Clark's with narrow fit and short skirt.

Angela was a very pretty and agreeable young woman and not stupid, and as she made great efforts in these directions she made friends, mostly men friends, in radio at first and later among TV people. She met boys who had film to sell, film by the mile, sometimes hijacked out of ONF stock, sometimes paid for by an indulgent parent in Outremont. After a while she found that she was seeing more French boys than English, which made her excited, content and prettier than ever.

Maplewood Avenue unveiled its charms to her. The street is in effect the dormitory of the Université de Montréal, since there is little residence accommodation on the campus. West from the Centre Social as far as Côte des Neiges, the street is a long row of apartments housing professors, students, and functionaries associated with university business. There is a certain amount of subterranean political activity carried on, usually in basement apartments rented by three or four students, providing each with low rent. These students are not rich. Many are poor, sometimes even hungry. They are older than the students Angela was used to and their interests are most various. They do not much like to speak English, and an English girl who speaks French is likely to seem an anomaly, perhaps to be taken up and examined with curious care, perhaps then to be put down.

She got a second-floor apartment on Maplewood just west of the campus and started to submit programme ideas to her producer which took her into the university *ambiance*. First one of her programmes got aired, then another; she learned how to make an acceptable tape under difficult conditions, huddled under a speaker's platform or in the cloakroom after a violent *conférence*.

I used to see her where I work, standing among the coffee and sandwich machines, talking rapid inaccurate French to students her own age, sometimes to a *chargé d'enseignement junior*, a writer or critic. She became rather well-known as a young woman who had made great strides, who might in the end manage to get all the way across. Then I heard that she was involved in the production of a half-hour film documentary for French TV, in which she was the star, interviewed in depth over several weeks in coffee houses, at work, *après-ski*, and the rest of it. When it was finally telecast the half-hour was called 'Miss Robinson', a Franglicism of the type which repels Général de Gaulle, like *le barman, le weekend*, prevalent in certain Parisian circles, and creeping into Montréal society.

I had the feeling that this title might have concealed immediately under the surface a certain puritanical, if playful, contempt, typical of many of the younger French intellectuals in the city. Sometime later I learned that Miss Robinson had changed her given names to 'Marie-Ange' pronounced with the strongly aspirated French 'r' which is almost an 'h'. Apart from stressing it like a French word, giving each syllable equal emphasis in an un-English way, she couldn't do much about 'Robinson'.

The TV film had a certain impact when it appeared on Canal Deux. Full of nuance, half mocking and half encouraging, it managed to suggest much of the ambiguity and pathos in the situation of the transformed Marie-Ange. She used that name in the interviews. Whether she had attempted something impossible was left an open question in the viewer's mind. She photographed beautifully; perhaps part of the joke was this vivid presentation of her new beauty which owed very much to, might indeed be said to derive from, purely French manners.

Certainly her circle of men considered her a beauty. Stéphane Dérôme had been floating around film circles for a couple of years, working first in amateur film, then for a time for an independent producer, then as composer of the score for an expensive feature, launched with much publicity, which sank without trace. He took her up lovingly, on the waves of the 'Miss Robinson' furore. She had become the mode.

In those days I was spending a lot of time out at the Montrose Record Centre on Bélanger, west of Montée Saint-Michel. As you come over from the centre of town, east on Jean-Talon or Bélanger, you'll be struck by the flatness and lack of charm of this neighbourhood. What is it, northern Rosemont or eastern City of Montréal? I've forgotten the boundary streets, if in fact I ever knew them. It's *calme plat, terne*, though you might be interested by the Italian neighbourhood between Papineau and D'Iberville, lots of *gelato* parlours and *sartorie*. On Papineau near Bélanger, there are two dozen brand-new multiple dwellings, quadruplexes and octoplexes inhabited by Italians who have made a few bucks since they got here; they may own a store, or four dump-trucks, or a gardening business – the city is full of Italian gardeners – in which they employ relatives, more recent arrivals.

These enormous new places they're living in, along Papineau, are built exactly like others all over the island, but the Italian ones somehow or other have an unmistakably Mediterranean air, very curious to discover in Montréal in the pale watery haze of early March, the snow melting, evaporating, obscuring the weak sun. It's the paint. They've all been painted in the most cheerful colours. Instead of brown brick and fake-modern light fixtures, you get yellow or white stucco or pink or electric blue, with plenty of enormous lamps in the wide windows.

This is certainly gay and distinctive, but when you are past the Italian strip, you're past the charm; the streets north and south no longer have names but numbers, First Avenue, Seventh Avenue, all the way out to the extreme east end, where Forty-fifth Avenue winds off into fields. In a city with a rue Mozart, rue Guizot, rue Dante, this dull system seems regrettable.

Around the Montrose Centre the buildings are drab new housing dating from the mid-fifties, with little to distinguish one from the next. It's surprising to find the record store in such a location because, as I once told the owner, George Tabah, it's 'the most exciting record store in town'.

He thought this over while I went through the Nonesuch bin, featured that day at a very good price.

'I may use that in an ad,' he said finally, 'I like it. "The most exciting record store in town".'

He never did use it though, whether because he didn't want to trust an amateur copywriter or because he advertises exclusively in *Le Devoir*. I think he places the ads by phone because they are oddly spelled, 'Brethen' for Britten, or 'Von Williams' for Vaughan Williams, surely the result of garbled telephone report.

'The most exciting' for two reasons: because you can get a fine classical selection at the best prices in town, and because the store is the principal centre for purchasers of discs by *les chansonniers* as well as a haunt of would-be or prospective *chansonniers*, live, in person, such as Stéphane Dérôme. In the display window underneath the perpetual announcement of a big sale VENTE DE DISQUES COLUMBIA BARCLAY FRANÇAIS ET JAZZ, are ranked dozens of display album covers of the great singers of the province: 'Le Nouveau Claude Leveillée', 'Pauline Julien á la Comédie Canadienne', 'Gilles Vigneault Chante'. Once at the very back of the window, dusty and less shiny than the other gaily coloured albums, there was a copy of Stéphane's first record, 'Stéphane Dérôme: Mon Coeur á Toi', oversha-

dowed by pyramids, circles, squares of 'Monique Leyrac: Pleins
Feux'. There was a lot of Leyrac promotion on a streamer,
'*Palmarès, concours international de la chanson*', and so on.

Sometimes when I was idling away a chilly early spring afternoon talking to George about the complexities of record mar-
keting, I would see Stéphane and Marie-Ange down at the end
of the narrow aisle, holding up for inspection first one record
then another. I could hear a continuous soft flow of critical
comment from them.

'Not the real thing.'

'Too much arrangement, do you think?'

'No, he is simply a poor poet. The music is not bad.'

Marie-Ange took most of Stéphane's comments at face
value, possibly because of his plan to become a *chansonnier* himself. You have to understand what this implies, and it's not
simple. In French Canada, since the seventeenth century,
there's been a great race of singers, a descending tradition, who
compose their own songs – that's the most important thing. A
Québec *chansonnier* is *not* a collector and performer of folk
songs, nor is he a popular entertainer; there is nothing primitive
about his work. He has to be a poet, a good musician, a performer on some instrument. Sometimes, like Gilles Vigneault,
he recites and acts things out. He must be a leader and
encourager of his people. In Québec now, there are three or
four magnificent singers of this kind, not more, and plenty of
would-bes.

In France the term means something a bit less serious, like
'singer-comedian-satirist', and here we move closer to the style
of Aznavour, or Jacques Brel, who does what is really a night-
club or theatre act. Brel sings, acts, writes, and in most respects
resembles a Québec *chansonnier* with the one great difference
that he doesn't have the responsibility to protect and encourage
the national tradition of a resentful minority. He has real gifts,
but not the same social commitment. 'Winter is my country,'
sings Gilles Vigneault, getting a strength that Jacques Brel can't
quite manage; of course, there is a difference in their audiences.
When Brel sings 'Ne me quitte pas', his impersonation of an
anguished lover can be recognized and appreciated anywhere in
the world. But this is nevertheless a commercial love song.

In my book Stéphane Dérôme had the talent of a minor film composer or a commercial songwriter, not that of a poet, an actor or leader. An accomplished pianist with plenty of formal musical training, certainly good-looking and pleasant to talk to, able to get through an acceptable evening on a guitar, he reeked of Paroisse Saint-Germain and of Stanislas, not at all of small isolated Natashquan-type villages eight hundred miles east. He played dates in small restaurants, made a record, was praised by his friends, by Marie-Ange, by Victorine Boucher who had starred in that doomed feature film he'd composed.

This group flocked to the Montrose Record Centre like the swallows in March, picking up disc after disc, buying many, discarding the unauthentic ones. They all seemed to know each other intimately, with the exception of Marie-Ange. She was always in the centre of the group, forcing the pace of the chatter a little hysterically, flushed. 'I knew that Stéphane was going to Québec for the weekend, and that Victorine would likely be there, so I had to think twice about asking Jacques to find out if Stéphane planned to be back in town for the Leclerc concert, because I'd have to make up an extra bed so that François could stay over. I know that Victorine knows that I know that Stéphane was there because she was, but *ça, ça m'est égal.*' At such times her eyes took on an earnest, hungry look. I began to watch the people with her, some of whom I knew, a contributor to *Cahiers AGEUM*, a boy preparing a volume for Editions Hexagone. They were kind to her, I thought, letting her run on as she pleased, rarely interrupting.

Her full flow of talk was assuming obsessive proportions, it seemed to me. Towards the end of March, I got a little extra money quite unexpectedly, which meant that for once I had enough money to gratify my need to buy records. I hustled out east, arriving at the Montrose about two o'clock, figuring on spending most of the afternoon talking to George and slowly and happily picking out forty dollars' worth of his bargains. I wasn't really happy to be interrupted in the middle of our conversation, which had developed through some long pauses over about an hour.

'Why don't you stock the Haydn Society reissues?'

Moments would pass slowly while he thought about this.

He went next door and brought back a pear from the fruit store, which he began to eat slowly and with relish.

'Well?'

'Why won't you pay more than two-fifty for a record?'

'Can't afford it. Get me Haydn Society at two-fifty or under and I'll gradually take the whole line.'

'Can't be done.'

'They do it in New York.'

We'd been over all this before, and we both started to laugh, and on the wave of our laughter Marie-Ange was carried in the door. She made straight for me and instantly began to talk as though we were the closest of friends, maybe even related, and as though in the middle of a sentence broken off seconds ago. Conversation with her was always exhausting for the first minutes, while you tried to figure out whom she was referring to and what was implied.

' – couldn't stand pets, any pets, so they had to go, as I couldn't consider moving, not right now with so much happening downstairs.'

'Downstairs?'

'In our building, Victorine's apartment. She claims there has been a voyeur peeking in the bedroom windows, she's right in the basement you know, and thinks it may be dangerous. If you ask me, it's Gérard up to some trick or other.'

'Voyeurism doesn't sound like Gérard. Satyriasis, more likely.'

'I wish some of it would rub off on me,' she said gloomily.

'Oh, come on.'

'Then again it could be François though he's still supposed to be in Québec.'

'It couldn't be Stéphane, I suppose?'

'I think it might, but then why go to all the trouble of peeking? He has full access to Victorine's apartment.'

'Oh?'

She had been just on the boiling point, simmering as it were, and now boiled over. 'Heaven knows I try,' she said, 'I do my best. *Je fais mon très petit possible, quoi?*'

'*Evidemment.*'

'What I have to put up with. I've been out with these guys

every night in the week for months; it's affecting my skin. I've put them on the air. I want an AM show where I can do bilingual interviews and meet people and try to help. And then to be told that I can't really be part of the group because I can't understand their jokes, it's something else, really. *Pas gentille.*'

'It's very hard.'

'What?'

'To catch the jokes. I speak a fair French myself and....'

'Pooh,' she said, 'pooh. A lot of it is smut, pure and simple, nothing but sex. Look at French theatre, intrigue, bare bosoms.'

'I'm in favour of that.'

'I can see you would be, but what woman can be bothered?' She glanced at George Tabah and moved to the back of the store; there was an unmistakable air of strain and ill-health about her. When I followed her back, she lowered her voice. 'There's something up that I don't know about, involving François and Gérard and Stéphane and Victorine, a plot of some kind, and I just can't keep up to what they're saying.'

'Not politics, surely?'

'No, no, nothing like that. You can't see Stéphane risking it, can you? No revolutions for him.' She had a Leo Ferré album in her hands and was examining his face with some bitterness.

'That's the stuff,' she said, 'Ferré, good and strong.'

'I find him a little hard to take.'

'You would.'

This was simply generalized resentment – at least I hope it was – and I let it pass.

'I'm sorry,' she said, 'I'm not your responsibility, am I?'

That question always bothers me, and I didn't answer.

'I've been so miserable,' she said.

George had left the store for a moment. He was standing outside with his back to the window, looking at the sky. The March light was extremely ambiguous, very pale, chilly looking, yet with a peculiar tone in some way evocative of the approach of finer weather. It was still plenty cold out, but another few weeks would see us out of it. The equinoctial gales, very troublesome in Montréal, had just begun, and the wind was gusting to fifty. And yet there was this almost imperceptible promise of fineness to come. The end of winter makes me feel better, encourages a certain buoyancy of feeling. Perhaps it had the reverse effect on Marie-Ange, and she was simply expressing physical discomfort induced by the weather. I said, 'Tell me about it, if you like.'

She gave a faint smile. 'You don't want to hear.'

'I'm not sure.'

'I'll tell you something anyway. I love Stéphane.'

I sometimes wonder whether there are any girls here and there burdening other men with the tale of their hopeless passion for me. The man who hears this story is bound to feel considerable distaste for the love-object, from feelings of unacknowledged rivalry perhaps; few men really care for the role of confidant. When she said this, I was conscious of a sharp pang of dislike for Stéphane. I felt like making a callous and flippant answer like, 'Sorry about that, chief,' but repressed the impulse. I said, 'He's a very nice guy,' thinking that, on the whole, he wasn't much.

Naturally Marie-Ange, far from stupid, sensed this, and putting down the Ferré disc she went out of the store more quickly, if anything, than she'd entered. You're a cold fish, I told myself. You might have been nicer. Must be the change in the weather.

When I heard about Victorine and Stéphane going off to Paris together, I kept my ears open and was able to collect a pretty full impression of the end of Marie-Ange's affair. Victorine, dark, small, fragile of ankle and wrist, adorable, had innocently announced that she would be in Paris for the principal event of the year, the opening at the Olympia of Claude Gauthier and Monique Leyrac. To such bait more considerable men than Stéphane Dérôme would have risen. They booked seats together on the appropriate Air Canada flight, Stéphane including his banjo and guitar and little else in his weight allowance.

He had a final meeting with Marie-Ange out at the Montrose, just checking over the new releases, I suppose. She turned to him with bewildered tears in her eyes, certainly incapable of understanding why she hadn't reached him.

'*Ne me quitte pas!*' she said.

'Brel,' said Stéphane absently, and he turned away.

Around Theatres

BY EASTER THE RINKS have melted, the hockey season is almost over, so you naturally switch to going to the movies. There's a driving vitality about early spring in Montréal that arouses actors and *cinéphiles* equally from hibernation in theatre school or *ciné-club*. The latter stop watching the Polish Film Festival every Tuesday night on Canal Deux and begin to circulate around the immense range of movie houses in the east end. The actors begin to think about new informal repertory companies in somebody's basement, often with the air of early Christian martyrs withdrawing to the catacombs.

It would be a misjudgement to confuse theatre people, particularly English ones, with film people, in these times much in the ascendancy. Movies are in the saddle and ride mankind.

So in mid-April, sun strengthening, bald brown patches looming on the mountainside above Fletcher's Field, tentative *tennismen* staring hopefully at sodden courts, I start catching up on the twenty important movies I missed fooling around on rinks all winter. The new Fellini, another Cassel-de Broca comedy, Godard reruns for one night only at the University. The European film menu is like good goulash, lots of meat and potatoes and a tart gravy. About the English and American output there's little to be said, and that harsh.

When Le Parisien opened near the statue of Edward the Peacemaker, three or four years back, I was dumbfounded to find that it was the French house farthest west in the city. I was a newcomer to Montréal then, and thought of Phillips Square with its convenient public lavatories and statue of King Edward as pretty far east, although the Main is nominally the dividing line. That bald greenish copper head – shining in light spring rain, pavement and sidewalk around him black reflectors of the shopping noon – King Edward always seemed to me to mark the penetration farthest east of the imperial style of life. I was the more surprised to find that no movie house had ever shown European pictures on a regular basis in the centre of the city.

What you get, along Ste-Catherine, are first-run houses like those you see riding a Greyhound bus through Buffalo, N.Y., showing surf epics, Disneys, and James Bond. Once in a long time, an English theatre on Sherbrooke West shows a fairly decent English picture, almost always a Woodfall Film, which means the Tush with her snaggle-toothed grins, *ad infinitum*. Apart from this, the English-speaking scene is bleak, unrelieved.

But from Le Parisien east, things are different, although Le Parisien itself failed in its original policy of bringing French movies downtown. When they opened, they got hold of a designer who did up the lobby in a reflection – at some distance – of Parisian café life, little tables in alcoves, ushers dressed as caped gendarmes, a pleasantly spurious impression was effected. But after two years the management announced they were going back to James Bond, Disneys, and surf epics because, they claimed, there weren't enough first-class French movies to programme, a palpable falsehood. At this point, luckily for them, they booked in Louis de Funes in *Le Gendarme de St-Tropez*, a sensational success with English shoppers because of the magnificent colour, the acres of skin on display, a richly farcical plot. It ran for months, and since then the house has been playing de Funes, de Funes and again de Funes, perhaps not a policy to redeem their hopes for long.

The big places in the mid-town shopping district have to book American movies with international stars; but as you go east past the Main, and north away from Ste-Catherine, you'll find dozens of French *cinémas* or Italian, exhibiting programmes of fantastic variety. They play to smaller and more discriminating audiences, they pay lower rental on the imported films, their patrons come from very distinct groups. I can think off-hand of four or five types of European *cinémas*; there are certainly more.

Somewhat like Le Parisien, for example, specializing in good first-run French comedies, is Le Dauphin, Beaubien près Iberville. The new de Broca is there now, and *L'Homme de Rio* was in for close to six months, making a flock of dough. This is a small neighbourhood house in a solidly Québécois district; it's immaculately maintained and draws from all over the east end.

A bit more on the arty side: Cinéma Festival, east on Ste-

Catherine somewhere around Chez Pierre, a commercial house which nevertheless schedules superior, perhaps slightly self-conscious, programmes by directors less immediately entertaining than de Broca (the poor, young, man's René Clair). Wait a minute, that's not strictly accurate, because *Peau de Banane* played there for God knows how long. Maybe they took it because Jeanne Moreau had the lead and Moreau, as everyone knows, is a serious actress, trained at the *Comédie*.

Then there is the struggling little Empire, *cinéma d'essai*, hidden behind the TV studios of Channel Twelve, on Ogilvy back of Jean-Talon. Older, drabber, smaller than these others, the Empire survives by running bargain double-bill revivals of very fine movies, a Truffaut retrospective or a Chabrol.

If you're just an ordinary moviegoer like me, who will watch anything and the worse the better, you can go to the Laval, just below Boulevard Mont-Royal on St-Denis, to watch double bills of French B-movies, the kind that art theatres in Toronto or New York never buy. You can catch up on the later work of Martine Carol if that's what you like (that's what I like), or maybe half-forgotten comedies starring Daniel Gélin or Pascale Petit, laughs and gentle sex.

Then there's the Saint-Denis, an enormous place on the street of that name, which shows big European musicals and which, because of its technical facilities and size, is the place to house a touring revue. When Annie Cordy and Luis Mariano come to the city biennially, they appear at the Saint-Denis, where they reap a rich harvest.

And finally, plinth, zenith, capstone of cinematic action in Montréal, there are the Cinématheque Canadienne, a tiny place on McGill St., and the Elysée, with its dual auditoriums, the Salle Resnais and the Salle Eisenstein. I've never been to the Cinématheque for the same reasons that I've skipped the Stratford Festival, but I've been around the Elysée quite a lot and am happy to praise it: the place where you can see *Une Femme Mariée* before it plays New York, which broke the local silent embargo on Godard films in general, the nesting place of Cacoyannis and Kobayashi, and Polanski, Buñuel. Shall I stop?

The upstairs auditorium where these films have their first

run, the Resnais, might seat 550, and the little ground floor room, the Eisenstein, 120. When *Le Bonheur* has played sixteen weeks upstairs and the receipts have fallen off, the management shifts it to the smaller room where it may survive another sixteen weeks. By the time a film has been through both houses, every enthusiast in town has seen it at least once and it's been squeezed dry, at least until some years have passed and it has acquired the dignity of a classic, when it may play the Elysée again or be relegated to a lesser *cinéma d'essai*.

Here one first saw *L'Année Dernière à Marienbad*, sat through a week of Renoir revivals, caught up at last with *The Magnificent Ambersons*, and in short cut one's cinematic teeth. In the small, irregularly shaped lobby with its unvarying exhibition of paintings by some execrable unknown, its orange drink and candy booth which also sells discs of songs from films, before the nine-thirty show one encounters the *gratin* of the city's amateurs of film: extravagantly slim young women, emaciated, short, with shining beautifully brushed caps of hair down to their brows, chattering with radical animation to their escorts, perhaps themselves film-makers or journalists or university people. You don't see many stage actors there.

I sneaked into the back of the ancient playhouse, long a movie theatre on the Main and now a training school for the stage, to watch Gus Delahaye at work, something I hadn't had a chance to do before. I shouldn't have been there but by a devious route known only to a few hundred friends of the company I had gained entry. I love old and disused movie theatres perhaps more than new ones in full flood of programming, the faded gilt on the box railings, the dusty velvet ropes, dark signs saying 'Loges', old framed stills and posters. This house was dark except on stage where Gus and five other students were rehearsing sword-play. Standing silently in the back, I felt like I was looking at TV with the sound down, which always reveals an enormous amount about an actor's control of his body. Of the men on stage, Gus certainly had the most skill in physical movement; he had a long, loose-jointed body, almost a dancer's, putting you in mind of Ray Bolger. He couldn't for the life of him establish a fluid smooth line with his limbs, all bones, knobs, joints. But as a comic puppet, he seemed to me to have great powers.

The instructor called from the house, 'You take Parolles, Gus,' and they all changed roles. As Parolles, Gus was perfectly cast. His movements with his sword inimitably suggested the combination of crafty braggart and shrinking coward, all over-statement and flourish without putting forward as much as a toenail. I thought he would make a fine Parolles, and in a highly specialized production might even rise to Iago. It would be a mime's Iago, of course, fantastic, as if masked, not a plain blunt honest fellow.

Thinking it over afterwards, Gus Delahaye seems to me to have been the most talented of the young men at the school over these last years. Without the physical endowments of the leading man, not at all a handsome, strongly built *jeune premier*, he had all the other gifts of the stage actor, an excellent voice, especially for comedy, with a wide range from a squeaky Punch to a growling Leporello. He could handle straight dialogue very well too, and had done some radio work in leading parts from which his physique otherwise debarred him.

He had a mobile, intelligent, hollow-cheeked face, and a thick shock of floppy brown hair worn long at back and side without affectation, simply as part of an actor's equipment. He was an enthusiastic planner of underground theatre move-ments, aimed at eventually doing down films and TV. He hoped for a regular, continuing, adequately financed experimental theatre, where he and other 'real' actors could develop their technique in new plays by people like me. Clown theatre, mime theatre, dance theatre in ensemble, chorus, duet, solo, with music, décor, new and profound and amusing dialogue. He hoped for much.

I met him through Seymour and Shvetz, and the first time the four of us were together we spent the night, or what was left of it, talking about the chances of having our own theatre.

It looked so pat to me. I kept on saying, 'A painter, a musi-cian, an actor, and me.' I may have been a little drunk. 'It fits. You paint the sets, Seymour. Sam plays the clarinet, the tam-bourine and the bagpipe. Gus and Julie act. And I....'

'What do you do?'

'Ideas and dialogue.' That was doubtless presumptuous, but afterwards whenever we got together Gus would stare at me hungrily and say, 'What about our theatre?'

Then one Sunday night I saw him work on a TV play, a half-hour show out of Montréal. He was not exactly featured, being used more as a prop, support, in a film-within-a-film. A pair of young lovers had a film to peddle to the CBC. The boy made it; the girl was in it. Gus played a Harlequin companion to the girl. He had no lines but was on camera for most of the show. I saw at once why he hated the film medium; he wasn't a screen actor and never would be. Seen at such close quarters, he seemed heavily made up, though as he told me afterwards he had worn almost none. His face was too big. I don't mean too big physically, but everything he did with his eyes and mouth would have been effective at stage distance and was quite grotesque when brought right into your living room, six feet from your chair.

Once I asked him, 'Why do you live on Guilbault?'

'Because it's convenient, near the school, and so forth.'

'Pure masochism,' I said.

'No, really.'

I said, 'Come off it. You live here because it's just up the street from the Elysée. You're nothing but a Jesuitical self-torturing actor.'

'Maybe it's true.'

'You know it is.'

Guilbault is a little street running east and west down near Milton and the Main, one block north of the Elysée. When there is an important new picture playing, cars and scooters are parked all the way from Clark and Milton to the corner of Guilbault. Crowds of moviegoers stream out of the cars and down the street, a perpetual irritant to Gus and Julie, to whose live performances few come, mostly friends. They have a first floor flat, corner Clark and Guilbault, with mattresses on the floor in the *salon* and an ambiguous oil lurking in the dim recesses of what might be the kitchen.

He said, 'What did you think of me on TV?'

'Strongest thing in the show, but you're not an actor at all, you're a mime. You ought to be in a circus.'

He winced, and I got that sinking feeling which means you've said something that's been said too often. When I was a small child being introduced to my parents' friends, or to strangers, I learned to shrink as they heard my surname, always eliciting, 'Any relation to Robin?' One time, I remember, meeting a mathematician named Whitehead, I observed fatuously, 'Not *the* Whitehead?' What a dirty look that man gave me. Brrr! There are times it's better not to try to be funny.

'They all say that,' said Gus violently, 'doesn't anybody ever really *think* about what comes out of his mouth?'

'It just popped out.'

'I'm not a mime. I'm an actor. An *ac-tor*. I have complete technical competence, in body movement, mime, voice, diction, vocal projection. I can manage small parts in passable French. I can do you almost any accent in spoken English, and not just a stage version either. I know something about modern linguistics, and I read verse beautifully. I can direct, work out a lighting plot, and in a pinch build flats. I know I'm not really suitable for films or TV, but that isn't acting at all; it's simply letting the director use your face like putty. Who needs that? Real acting, that's stage acting, distance, makeup, costume, artifice.'

'You're preaching to the converted.'

'I'm not talking to you. This is what we in the theatre call a *tirade*. Grand, isn't it? I can go on for hours.'

'I hope you won't.'

'One thing more, you're damned right, I hate the Elysée and the damned stupid bloody crowd that goes there. Not because they're French (Julie is half French), and anyway half of them are English phonies dressed up like French intellectuals. I hate them because of all this nonsense about the movies. Do you realize that I can't get any work in Montréal? None.'

'It's as bad as that?'

'You're a fool.'

'But I'd be glad to come and see you work. The thing is, live theatre may be a dying form.' I said that out of pure orneriness and it had the desired effect. He began to leap about the room like a wild stallion. Really. I had the impression he was miming a wild stallion without being aware of it. The snorting was tremendous.

'It is not a dying form. There's plenty of live French theatre in the city. It's just all you awful lard-bottomed, stay-at-home moviegoing bourgeois nothings.'

When I hear the word 'bourgeois', I know the conversation is over, so I picked up some papers I'd brought along and prepared to leave. I said, 'Good-night, Mrs Delahaye.' I hadn't known them long.

She said, 'Miss Brittain,' very sour.

'Oh, sorry, good-night.'

He had a grievance, you've got to admit. I don't know why there isn't any English theatre here. I'm no apostle of the theatre. I don't believe all this Tyrone Guthrie crap about how a society *needs* a theatre if it's to be truly great. There was no theatre among the Jews during the Exodus – see what I mean? It's a dispensable institution, and to hell with it. Except that on the whole you get the feeling that English Montréal – not about to cross the Red Sea – has the means to support a theatre and is just too mean to do it, too small and too perverse.

After that we spent many evenings planning our theatre. It would be very small but would pay the company and the director a more than nominal wage, enough to live on decently, surely not an uneconomical requirement. I would be the unpaid (I have large private means) resident dramatist, at first providing only suggestions for improvisations and occasional short passages of dialogue for rehearsal purposes, learning how to distinguish characters by the sound of their speech patterns, as well as by the sense of what they say, not an easy trick. We would do programmes about an hour long, comprising three or four exercises in free theatre: ten minutes of silent mime or clowning on situations suggested by me, then maybe a quarter of an hour of spoken improvisation, then a rehearsed and memorized scene for two actors, played through twice with the actors reversing their characterizations, finally perhaps a short passage from one of the classics. About an hour in all, plenty of variety.

We would sell tickets, have a business manager – the more we planned, the more complicated the thing became, even with such modest production ambitions. We thought of running each programme two weeks.

Julie, a bit of a carper, said, 'Are there enough intelligent people in Montréal to keep us running two weeks?'

'How many seats would we have? Do we have to get a licence and pay entertainment taxes?'

Gus always got very riled up when we raised these humdrum points. Looking back, I see that he never had any intention of realizing this fantasy, very Canadian, that. At a sad complete dead end in his own work, for purely practical reasons not his fault, he must have been living in a state of chronic frustration close to paranoia.

The only experimental evening that materialized out of our plans must have been the final disillusionment. It was mid-April. We decided to take the leap and work up our first programme, using the Delahaye-Brittain living room as the playing area. It was quite a large room when the mattresses were rolled back. I invented some ideas for improvisations; some theatre school types were to act them out, testing various mime techniques and trying out dialogue. After making notes on what came out, I was supposed to go home and write up short scenes for later rehearsal on the basis of what evolved.

I was really charged up for the occasion. I mean, here we all were, taking the step that might long afterwards go some way towards freeing our theatre (if we absolutely have to have one) from dependence on the dramatic literature of other times and places. I didn't, you understand, plan to become a great new dramatist, but I thought I might be one of the middling ones who get things rolling.

Besides Gus and Julie and me, there were three actors present. Gus was fuming and pacing up and down. 'It's not enough. Eight or nine promised to come. We need variety, lots of different approaches.'

'It's enough to get started,' said one of the other guys, a fellow named Joe D'Amico, a young leading-man type, but without Gus's versatility and technique. The others were beginners at the school who'd obviously turned up out of curiosity and possibly the wish to get in with an older crowd. Neither showed much spark, and both were very self-conscious.

'O.K.,' said Gus decisively, 'we've got four men and a girl. Later we'll have to get at least one more girl, but we can do something tonight. Give us an idea to get started.'

'This involves two men,' I said, 'we'll talk it over and rough in the implications. Then you can play it, improvising the speeches. Afterwards two others can have a go.'

'What about me?' said Julie.

'Why not be the director for now? Block it out with them, give them some moves.'

'So what's the situation?' said Gus eagerly.

I looked around. 'We really don't have the right physical types for this, but that's good, we can compensate for it. There are two men, both in love with the same girl. One of them is around twenty-two, a juvenile, kind of a Jean-Louis Trintignant type. The other is in the mid-to-late forties, charming, rich, experienced. He's more or less taken the girl away from the young chap for a while, but now he sees that he's too old for her and that she really loves the other guy. He's on the point of admitting this, and giving them his blessing, sort of. The juvenile doesn't realize this – maybe he's a bit slow on the uptake – and he's ready to fight. This scene comes well on towards the end of the play, and it should have an autumnal tone.'

'It sounds like a Jean Gabin vehicle. It's banal.'

'All situations are banal, it's a question of what you make of them. Let's try this and see what happens.'

Julie took over. 'Joey, you be the young man, and Gus the older one.' She asked me, 'Does the older one know the young one wants to fight?'

I said, 'You're doing the improvising.'

'I think he does,' she said, thinking it over. She gave the experiment a real good try, the best of any of us. 'I think he knows the young guy is on the point of slugging him, and though he's made up his mind to hand the girl back – what kind of bitch is she anyway – he doesn't want to be intimidated. He tries to keep control of the situation.'

'So, go on.'

'Do we give them names?' She suggested names which didn't sound quite right to me, and I'd have changed them if I'd ever written the scene out. She gave a lot of direction, and then we all sat down against the wall to watch what came out.

Nothing.

I always believed it would happen, but it didn't. Having seized their freedom, they could do nothing with it. They wandered around, putting their hands in their pockets and taking them out, and staring at each other foolishly.

Julie said, 'What's the matter?'

'Uh,' they said together, scared to death.

'Come on, flog your imagination. Gus, put some weight on, walk like a rich man, you can do that.' But he couldn't. In a few minutes they sat down disgustedly and gave the others a chance. They were no better, couldn't invent any lines.

'I was going to adapt your ideas,' I said, 'but there's nothing to adapt.'

'Ah, nuts,' said Gus, 'the situation was lousy.'

'Oh, it was not,' said Julie. She was very upset. We all began to argue, then to quarrel, and in short nothing came of the project. When the others had gone home, Julie and I sat with Gus for quite a while, consoling him.

'Anyway, it's a beautiful night,' I said, 'there's nothing like April in Montréal.'

'So you're one of those saps that lets the weather affect you? Christ, man, the weather isn't good or bad, that's simply the pathetic fallacy, don't you even know that? It's all in your emotions, the universe doesn't give a damn about you.' He was very disturbed. 'Besides, God is dead.'

'I don't think so.'

'What do you know about it, any more than anybody else?' I could have made some answer, but it would have taken a long time.

At the end of the month, I got a call from Julie, half in tears. 'Gus has disappeared. I haven't seen him for over a week and this time I'm really afraid something has happened. Last time I saw him was around midnight, a week ago Sunday. He suddenly got out of bed, right in the middle too. He said he was going to plant a bomb in the phone booth beside the Elysée box office. Then he went out and nobody's seen him since. Can you think of anything?'

'Have you talked to the cops?'

'No. I thought I better not in case he'd done something

foolish.' She was in a bad way, and it made me mad. What was so big about him that he had to run off? I drove over and tried to reassure her, saying that he likely preferred to keep a whole skin, like the rest of us.

In the end, of course, he couldn't stay away from our favourite restaurants, and was soon spotted sneaking in and out of this one and that one, carrying lean smoked meats to his cab for dinner.

'There's a lot of demand for a good, cautious cab-driver,' he said, last time I rode with him. 'At this I can always make a good living. Well, at least a living.'

Le Grand Déménagement

SUPPOSE YOU MOVE HERE the end of August, say. You arranged with your *propriétaire* for a lease which, no matter what your wishes, will terminate on April 30th the next year, or more probably the year after, giving you a *terme de bail* of twelve plus eight, or a total of twenty months. A lease in Montréal ends on April 30th. Useless to plead its inconvenience, if you only mean to stay nine months, or fifteen, because the custom is invariable. So God ordained it; so it remains.

That might sound like an exaggeration to a stranger, but in fact the custom of the great move on May Day is rigorously – I won't say enforced, there is no constitutional or legal prescription – but enjoined by immemorial habit. This has something to do with elements profoundly rooted in our people, a trust in the value of building, solid brick and mortar, the rental property. Sociologists assert that the impulse rises from the defensive instincts of a conquered minority. I don't believe that. I don't think any true Québécois ever resigns himself to such a status. This urge to acquire property is a constructive and aggressive force, not purely defensive. I can remember Professor Bonbourgeois, the economist, saying to me, 'Put your money in duplexes, my boy. Nothing is so good an investment.' And this man is very very far from being a minority-group defeatist. He's an aggressive and daring leader whose debatable pronouncements make members of the cabinet tremble and grow pale.

'Put your money in duplexes. Be paid rent. Grow fat.'

The *rentier* psychology is easy to understand, but where did the choice of April 30th (coincidentally my birthday, more about that later) originate? I've seen the question argued each year in the papers; nobody seems to know. It might have some quasi-ritual function. I suspect it does, something associated with the return of fine weather, the final long-deferred and patiently awaited coming of spring. The first of May is associated in many local devotional practices with the Mother of God, just as May is her month. Could there be something

going on here that nobody has noticed, an assimilation of the
new, unexplored and therefore slightly alarming domicile to the
protection of Mary? I'm not sure.

The movers in Montréal have for years been trying to push
through some modification of this practice of doing all the
moving on April 30th and May 1st. You can see the complica-
tions for them. I mean, think it over. Over 70 percent of their
business is done in a ten-day period at the end of April, when
you can't get hold of a mover for love or money unless you got a
signed agreement months before, when you can't under any circumstances rent a truck. All reserved, booked up solid. The
movers claim that they're in a ruinous business; they have to
maintain equipment the year round at a level of investment
only justified during the magical transformations of midnight,
April 30th, when old *foyers* die painfully and the new are born.
There's a suspicion of witchery about the whole rite.

What I want to know is this: what do the movers do the rest
of the year, hibernate? Do they sit around in an enchanted
slumber eleven months of the twelve, occasionally walking out
zombie-style to handle an industrial move? And how the hell
does it all work out so neatly without any displaced tenants left
over? I worry about this, looking at it as an enormously sophisticated problem in statistics and operations analysis.

Sixty thousand families load their furniture into trucks,
buses, station wagons, human- and horse-drawn carts, on April
30th, which means that there have to be sixty thousand open
spaces waiting. But these spaces are still occupied by sixty thousand others who are waiting for the first ones to get out, so they
in turn can occupy vacated space. No signal is given, like the
whistle at the kickoff, to warn half of the populace to move out
so that the other half can move in, permitting those already out
on the street to move in ... the mind boggles at the complexity
of the operation.

I've always been haunted by the spectre of the last man to
vacate, who at 11:59 on the night of May 1st, when everybody
else is happily settled in, dust falling back to the surface of newly
arranged bric-à-brac, finds himself wandering through the
streets of Montréal with all the spaces taken, as in musical
chairs. Some enchanter has sneaked in and removed one

apartment and there he is, the final tenant, seeking a home.

You may object that each year new apartments come into being, but equally each year are older ones demolished. There may be a small net gain in units available, but you can't tell me that the whole undertaking isn't wildly risky, like kicking over an anthill. One of these years the movers will get everybody out in the streets and then find that a hundred buildings have unaccountably vanished, leaving the whole transition irrecoverably muddled. The city will then become the habitation of nomads, eternally condemned to wander up and down Maplewood or Saint-Urbain, looking for a ghostly four-and-a-half with garage, locker, taxes paid, heat supplied.

This conception alarms me deeply each time I'm forced to consider moving, something I'd put off for the remainder of life's allotted span, if at all possible. Whenever my lease gets down towards the end of the final year, say six months before, I begin to scan the document nervously. Finally, obsessed by the complexity of the whole nightmarish undertaking, I contact my landlord months before there is any need, begging him to renew and undermining my bargaining position, so as to assure myself of three tranquil birthdays without another move.

The last time we actually had to do it, I worried, my wife worried. In November we began to review the 'Duplex to Let' columns and quite soon found one that was going to become available the end of February! Hallelujah. Now this meant that I paid rent on two apartments through March and April, but the peace of mind was worth it. Early in March we began to trans-ship stuff from the old to the new place, taking our time, after all we had nearly ten weeks. I used to load up our Volkswagen bus with junk from the locker, superannuated stuffed animals, picture frames, cartons of obscure and long-forgotten electrical devices, curling-irons and broken toasters. Three bicycles. I carried out and in, by my accurate count, thirty-two sixty-pound cartons of books. Then there were the records....

By my birthday we'd been in our new place for three weeks; God, but I felt smug. But on mulling it over, I see that I devoted a couple of hundred hours to the move; and figuring my time as worth a dollar an hour, approximately the local minimum wage, I didn't save as much as I thought.

But as I leaned back in my dining-room chair, took a deep breath and blew out the candles, I thought that after all we were relocated awfully conveniently, while at that very instant all the streets of the *métropole* were crawling with insect-like totings of heavy bundles. *Fourmillante cité*: bet your sweet life.

In our house we celebrate all conceivable festivals, the kids see to that. The Jewish high holidays are very big with us, though we aren't Jews. When you work it out, we have a major celebration every second week: Christmas, New Year's, Grandma's birthday, John's birthday, Valentine's Day, Lincoln's birthday because he freed the slaves, Saint Patrick's Day, Sarah's birthday, Easter, Dwight's birthday, taking us down to the end of April which is me.

Sarah came in one time from the parish school and announced 'Today is the feast of Saint Louise de Marillac.'

'Yeah,' I said, not too interested, 'so what about it?'

'Aren't we going to have a cake?'

I thought it over. 'I don't think Saint Louise de Marillac is close enough we have to have a cake.'

'Oh, Daddy.' She went off and took the matter up with her mother who, I'm glad to say, supported me in the issue.

So when I admit that I enjoy my birthday party, it isn't wholly from infantilism, it's really for the kids. We have party hats, the same ones we've used for everybody's birthday since Sarah was born, noise-makers, and those things that you blow into and they unroll with a whistling sound, a feather at the end to tickle your dinner partner's nose. After the first course is over – the kids don't eat much – we turn out the dining-room lights and Noreen goes for the cake. She brings it down the hall, we all sing, the candles are blown out, the cake is cut and then there are the presents. Everybody knows how the feast develops, even the baby. Everybody gets the same intense pleasure from repeating the same sequence of actions regularly at the same time each year. Just like a secular liturgy.

Part of my birthday party that the kids aren't aware of is my annual late-evening tour of the streets to observe the movers and their problems, not entirely a sadistic enterprise. Full of cake and striped ice cream, glad not to be loading a van, I wander out after the children are in bed to see how things are coming on; the activity continues late into the night all the next day.

An apartment, a *foyer*, grows an essence of its own as people live their way into it through the term of a long lease. It isn't just so many walls, so much raw physical space; the soul of the place is in the forming actions of its inhabitants – these are the true *lares et penates*. It is always sad to see so many patterns being broken all at once. Remember how you did things when you lived on South Drive? There was that peculiar low ceiling at the landing on the back stairs as you go up to the attic, where your wife always used to bang her head, carrying laundry baskets down from upstairs. You had a garage full of gardening tools such that you couldn't get the car in out of the winter weather. Your eldest boy, now in college, drew all over the living room walls at eighteen months, and you made the mistake of hanging new wallpaper yourself. Remember how sticky the paste was, and how you howled with laughter when the project had finally gotten out of rational control?

End-of-April night, ten o'clock along Maplewood, families leaving, taking a last look around to see if they've forgotten anything. They have, but they won't find out for weeks.

'What happened to that fruit jar, the one I used to save pennies in?'

'Didn't you put it in the carton with the ashtrays, when you were cleaning out your study?'

'I thought I did, but I can't find it. I had thirty-seven cents in there. I know because I wanted to roll them up and didn't have enough. *N'importe.*'

I come mooching along the street, watching them go, feeling each backward glance. A young father comes out of 2225 Maplewood holding a canary in a cage, with a sleepy three-year-old girl clinging to his leg, almost tripping him. Further along, where we used to live, there's a studio couch sitting beside some garbage cans. Somebody has abandoned it and my wife would swear that it was almost new. I sit on it and bounce, wondering if I should go home and get out the car and pick it up. Scavenging like this, we've acquired a house full of interesting pieces.

Have you ever tried to throw away a worn-out studio couch? I mean really worn-out, with the ends bulging out and the springs down to the floor? Can't be done! You have to wait till you move, or are fleeing the country under a cloud, to dispose of the item. We had one around the house so long it started to go bad – it smelled. I think mice were living in it. With immense difficulty, I and a pal wrestled the thing onto the balcony and tipped it over, hoping it would divide on impact so the garbage men would haul it away.

But it didn't. We had to work it into the bus and drive to an open space miles across town, safe from detection, as we hoped. We drew up on a slight incline, hauled the damned thing out, and left it settling cosily into the mud beside a baseball diamond.

'Coast away,' my buddy said.

For days I went skulking around nervously, expecting a call from the Sanitation Department charging me with trespass, littering, abandonment, whatever the formal accusation is. Better to leave them around your old apartment when you leave.

When we moved away from Maplewood, I sent the others off with the van and stayed behind for ten minutes with a broom, meaning to leave everything tidy. I swept up, borrowed a dustpan and emptied the sweepings into the incinerator, took a last look around at the four and a half empty rooms (five if you count the dining alcove as a room). Motes of dust danced in slanting sunbeams. In that corner, there, Sarah sat for hours with her crayons making Christmas or Easter cards. Here in the kitchen was where Dwight cried for six hours one night, causing my wife and me to have our worst-ever fight. Dwight was long past that stage now. Sarah would never sit in that corner again; the apartment seemed haunted by actions irrecoverably lost. What is permanent, I wondered? Where did all that go? Once on a birthday night walk, I counted seventy-four moving vans along Saint-Urbain in half an hour. Think what is lost forever in all this.

Especially on Saint-Urbain do you get the impression of the evanescence of life. From Van Horne south past Rachel, the street must have the highest population density in town, thousands of small apartments in two- and three-storey buildings, a balcony for each apartment, from which soft voices buzz on dark spring nights. It's an old quarter and some of the buildings are untrustworthy. Once last year, just before moving day, a young woman fully nine months pregnant was sitting with her grandmother on a Saint-Urbain balcony when all at once it pulled away from the face of the building and they fell three storeys to the ground. They were rushed to the Hôtel Dieu, fortunately not far off, and the miraculously unhurt young mother gave birth to a healthy infant, despite her understandable state of shock. I have the impression her grandmother wasn't quite so lucky.

On May Day, right after this unhappy accident, I was driving slowly past the place where it happened, looking in amazement at the raw scar on the front of the building. I stayed in second gear because of the crowds of trucks and other wheeled vehicles. Suddenly I saw an ancient man, bearded, standing in the gutter looking at a homemade wagon piled high with household effects, mattresses, bedding, pots and pans, half a ton of stuff. He had apparently meant to drag this weight unaided across the district to his new home, like a cart-horse in the traces. But his intentions had been dashed by the collapse of the wagon. A wheel lay at a crazy angle near the curb, a ragged stump protruding at the end of the axle. His effects teetered gently on top of the wagon.

This man wore the most puzzled expression I've ever seen. Not angry, not despairing, simply puzzled, as though he were working out a complex equation in his head.

My Volks bus was empty. I felt a compassionate impulse, struggled with it, almost crushed it down, but then stopped and got out, meaning to offer to help. We could easily have put his stuff in the bus and moved it in one load. I spoke to him but he apparently didn't understand me. I guess he was a Polish Jew. I began to wave my arms, pointing at my bus. A look of profound suspicion spread over his face, making me feel foolish in front of a considerable group of bystanders. I'm no good Samaritan or anything like that. I just figured what the hell, I had nothing else to do that afternoon.

As I stood there trying vainly to reassure the old man, another bearded figure materialized and seized me by the arm.

'That's a nice truck you got there, Meester,' said this man.

'It's not a truck,' I said, 'it's a station wagon.'

He looked with contumely at my scarred and dirty car. He knew what a station wagon looked like, and this was not it. 'By me it's a truck,' he said. 'You want to help me?'

I was certainly not getting through to the old fellow with the busted wagon, so I seized the chance to ease out of the situation.

'All right,' I said, trying to ignore the laughing crowd, 'what's your problem?'

'Two dollars.'

'Huh?'

'I'll give you two dollars.'

'No,' I said, 'I'm not in the moving business. Just tell me what you want.'

This affected his composure slightly. 'I want to move a sink. It's my tenant Swackhammer, oh my, you should have such a tenant, always complaining. It's got a crack; it leaks into the garbage pail and through the floor. He won't be responsible for the plaster, so I got to fix it.'

'A sink?' I visualized something you'd wash your hands in, a little bowl about eighteen inches across. 'Sure, I'll give you a hand.'

'So come.'

I followed him. He wore a heavy overcoat inappropriate for the season but easy to keep in sight, deep black. We entered a cavernous foyer and went up three flights of stairs into an enormous apartment running the length of the building and overflowing with all varieties of highly coloured furniture; there were framed photographs on all sides.

My employer waved a hand at the pictures. 'He gets them wholesale from a nephew, a druggist. The sink is back here.'

We went into the kitchen and there it was. I had been quite wrong in my estimate of its size. It was a bloody old battleship of a kitchen sink, divided in halves, one shallow for dishes, one deep for laundry. It was colossal, stained, cast-iron, and it sure was cracked. A deep fissure ran down the division between the tubs and across the bottom of the laundry tub; leakage might certainly occur.

'I'm simply protecting my property,' the man said.

'You own the building?'

'A small thing, a nothing,' he said evasively.

'How are we going to get this thing out of here?' It must have weighed over a hundred pounds and looked an awkward shape to move.

'Down the back. Go get the car and bring it round the alley.' I figured this man was used to exercising a certain amount of authority, saying to one 'Go,' and he goeth, and to another 'Come,' and he cometh; he had a basilisk eye. As it turned out, he was a rabbi and a scholar besides being a property owner, and something in his manner commanded assent, and anyway I was feeling easy. 'Bring it along Saint-Cuthbert and down the alley. I'll stand on the back balcony and stop you.'

I had to laugh; he had it all set up. I went downstairs and out to the street. The old Polish waggoner was nowhere to be seen, but his belongings were highly visible all over the street and in the gutter. Children were picking up the pieces. I got into my car and wheeled it slowly up the street, round the corner onto Saint-Cuthbert and down the first alley. Soon I saw an over-coated figure standing on the balcony, well back against the wall, away from a rickety railing.

'Stop, that's it.' He beckoned and climbed the stairs again, feeling it in my legs. Tenants began to appear at windows to watch our descent, which was difficult. A very fat woman leaned out of a second-floor window and cried angrily, 'Ha, Pachsman, I see you're fixing up Swackhammer's place.'

'A minor repair, that's all, a little porcelain job.'

'So what about the bugs?'

'They're being taken care of; it's no problem.'

'Sure they're being taken care of, but who's taking care of us? It's time you did something for me. Just because I don't complain, like some....' Her voice trailed off angrily as we went lower. I had the bottom end of the sink, the heavy end, and at that the Rabbi was doing a lot of huffing and puffing. When we finally got the damned thing into the car, he climbed into the back beside it and began to give me directions.

'It's over on Saint-Grégoire past the park. Drive fast. You can go along Saint-Urbain and across Laurier.'

'All right, all right. What's the hurry?'

'Swackhammer,' he said moodily.

We drove east on Laurier and north to Saint-Grégoire, then east again behind the park, a part of town I hadn't seen before. In a few minutes he told me to stop beside the entrance to what looked like an old stable; there was a high, weathered board fence around it, and around the yard an L-shaped ramshackle two-storey loft. We leaped out and entered the yard. I noticed a sign saying ROSEMONT PLOMBERIE, RÉPARATIONS, SERVICE. In a minute a foreman came out onto a platform on the second floor and lowered a length of chain with a hook on the end, meanwhile giving us elaborate directions. I had to back the car into the yard; then we had to lead the chain through the hole in the bottom of the sink on the good side. Then we had to work the hook through a link in the chain so the sink could be hauled up. It took a certain amount of time and energy, but finally we both heaved sighs of relief as this incubus was swung up into the sky above us and into the workshop. I turned to go, but Rabbi Pachsman had the last word.

'You're driving me home?' He had me there.

Next Monday night about twenty to six, I was eating supper with the family when the doorbell rang downstairs and the front door was flung resoundingly open. I stuck my head into the stairway and by God there he was, overcoat and all. I hadn't given him my address, and I still don't know how he found me. The car was parked outside. Could he perhaps have checked all the streets west from Saint-Urbain, looking for it, or did he simply take the licence number and check it with the Bureau?

'Meester, Meester, we gotta go quick, they close at six.'

'The sink, you mean?'

'What else?'

I hadn't said anything about any return trip.

'Besides I haven't given you the two dollars.'

'Oh, hell,' I said to my wife. 'Keep the coffee on the stove and I'll be back in an hour.'

Driving across Van Horne towards the east end, he kept bouncing up and down like butter in a fry-pan. 'Faster, faster.'

'Look, I can't go any faster, this is a street full of traffic.'

'They close at six,' he said in anguish, 'and Swackhammer....'

'Yeah,' I said, 'I know. Swackhammer is complaining.'

'You got it,' he said, 'faster, faster, go east on Saint-Grégoire.'

'Yeah, yeah, yeah.'

We made it about one minute to six, and he hopped out and ran into the old barn and upstairs. In a minute I heard loud contentious voices which rose in pitch; then his dominated, the chorus died away, and very shortly the re-porcelained sink was swung out overhead and lowered. I stood at a prudent distance until it touched ground. Then we unhooked it, stuck it in the back and had a look at it. They had certainly done a lovely job on the porcelain. It looked like a new fixture.

'Did they fix the crack?' I said. You certainly couldn't see it.

'That I can't say,' he said.

We drove back to his place in relaxed and comradely silence, and when we had carried the thing to the third floor, again to the jeers of the tenants and in the inexplicable absence of Swackhammer (could he possibly have been a polite fiction?), Rabbi Pachsman drew a long black purse from the depths of his overcoat and extracted a crisp new two-dollar bill.

'For you.'

'Aw, no, look, I'm not in the business. It was just a favour.'

He stuffed it into my shirt pocket.

'All right,' I said, 'I'll send it to a charity, B'nai B'rith or the Knights of Pythias.' He smiled cagily. I did send off the money too, I think to the United Jewish Appeal, but somehow I'm sure he'd never believe it.

Since then I park the car off the street.

Looking Down From Above

FAIR WEATHER implies heightened perception in my book. Once in early June, clear, hot and dry, intense yellow Montréal sunlight topped with blue, no clouds, I came down the west side of University south of Sherbrooke towards the crowded fenced stinking Eaton's parking lot, construction on the road ahead, knotted clumps of honking cars to my left, and the unprepossessing black marble and grey stone walls of an office building leaning over the sidewalk on my right. The road sloped downwards.

This is a murderous neighbourhood; the streaked, grey-stone building houses the head office of a locally held insurance company. The stone facing is drab and the fake black marble reflects ambiguous images. The sidewalk gets little sun here. Along Sherbrooke and south towards President Kennedy lie gutted shells and piles of rubble reminiscent of Berlin in 1945. Subway construction has passed this way, and unlovely unfinished apartment blocks jut up from the ruins, threatening a dubious future.

The ugliness of Eaton's held my eyes, that and the dismal push of cars towards Ste-Catherine, making my steps reluctant though the slope urged them. The concentrated dry heat stimulated feelings of mortality and a sense of the passage of time. I thought how this slope must have been without concrete or asphalt or monolithic department store, wire fence, diggings in the roadway, when deer ran on the mountain and silence began a hundred yards north of the river.

Coming slowly towards me, dragging her way up University, was a small old woman, almost a dwarf; this was the first time I ever noticed her though I often saw her afterwards. She moved with hesitant steps, placing one foot eight inches in front of the other, and she leaned in under the wall at an angle as if deformed in some way, in the left shoulder or neck. Our approach was slow, and for some reason I examined her carefully. It was like looking at a snapshot in a dream; the details of her appearance were extraordinarily sharply outlined and seemed pregnant with unstated meaning.

She wore small old club-like, run-over boots, splayed and worn through at the outside of the foot, scuffed. Coarse pale brown cotton stockings hanging in folds on shrunken calves, a brown dress which might sometime or other have been designed for a taller and younger person, with a row of twenty little black buttons the size of peas down the front to a loose belt. There was no question of the dress fitting her. Over it, on this hot day, she wore a man's light woollen topcoat perhaps thirty years old, hanging open almost to her ankles. In her right hand she clutched a worn purse, and from the left dangled a brown paper shopping bag with some heavy object at the bottom.

She came on and I walked slower and I saw her face, sunken and without teeth, colourless, deeply lined, her hair thick and stringy under what looked like a black cotton handkerchief, the eyes very bright and protruding like small ripe olives. She mumbled to herself. She was between seventy-five and eighty, I suppose, perhaps older, and she was alone. She kept coming.

Here, I thought, is somebody who has had to renounce all human pretensions to health, beauty, sexuality, earnings, and apparently even companionship. I wondered how she lived and what she ate, whether she took pleasure in her food and her life, what kept her going. We passed and our eyes met; there was fury in her eyes and extraordinary purpose. I could hear her words and felt afraid. She was full of life.

That woman am I. To her state must I come in time. I stood on the squalid street looking at her and wondering if she would speak to me, labouring under a drastic perception of the human soul in her, impenetrable and indissoluble. Then she passed slowly up the hill and I turned downwards wondering to what purposes she gave her concentration. At the corner I turned back and saw her standing on the top of the rise by Sherbrooke waiting for the green light.

You can't get too close, learn their names, start talking to them, or you become irrecoverably committed. Take Monsieur and Madame Bourbonnais, what were they to me when we came to Montréal? The concierge in our apartment building and her industrious husband; that was all. That was all. Mme Bourbonnais was in her mid-fifties, I guess, and a terribly pretty vivid woman. She had a beautiful head of thick wavy red hair, dyed, but dyed smartly and attractively. She used to talk to our children and teach them a word or two of French. She looked after the afternoon newspaper delivery on our block, handling delivery-boy absenteeism by the dignified and simple expedient of taking the route herself, with a little coaster wagon. She was always working, always happy and kind.

Her husband was a wiry little man about the same age. I doubt whether he ever weighed more than a hundred and twenty-five pounds. In effect, he had two full-time jobs, working a long daily shift as a shipper in a meat-packing plant way out in the east end, and as the building superintendent at our place on Maplewood, across from the delightful woods, and the paths, leading up to the University. He was always responsive to pleas for assistance at nights or on the weekend, a blocked sink, some defective electric outlet. He had a lot of plumber's and electrician's and carpenter's equipment, and was handy with it. We got so we didn't like to ask him to fix something, he was so obliging and so busy. Balding, with a fringe of still black hair over his ears, with light step and great energy, he always would come when you needed him. He used to laugh kindly about my French and taught me much.

When he wasn't fixing things in his spare time, he worked on one of his personal collections or projects. Once he showed me his scrapbooks of hockey pictures, and we talked for two hours down in the garage about the vanished greats of *Le Canadien*. Another time I asked him why he went through the garbage and collected all the newspapers and magazines. He said that he sold the magazines for a fraction of a cent a copy to second-hand dealers. The newspapers he rolled and tied in bundles of twenty-five pounds apiece, and sold them for re-pulping, twenty-five cents a bundle, a cent a pound. His workshop was usually piled high with these bundles, amounting in all to ten or twelve dollars' worth. For working in the apartment building, he got his rent, light and heat free and a small wage, and some Christmas gifts.

When this man bought his first car, a new Corvair, during

our stay in the building, he paid cash for it. I never saw anyone work harder for his pleasures or enjoy them more. He used to take his family for outings in the new car, leaving at seven or eight o'clock Sunday morning and coming back around eleven at night. He and Madame and their two sons would be laughing and talking excitedly; they might have done some fishing up in the Laurentians over towards Saint-Donat.

The boys were great big guys a foot taller than their father. One was a qualified optometrist with an office east on Boulevard Mont-Royal, and the other was at Hautes Etudes Commerciales and doing well. They were extremely polite men. Several times when my wife was unloading a week's groceries with a child under either arm – quite a trick – one or the other of the boys came and held doors and carried cartons and otherwise helped her out. The whole family were immensely dignified, respecful of each other and of other people, without being in any way oppressed by convention. They had a free, independent life together.

They were great on picnics, things like that, which they could enjoy together. It was M. Bourbonnais who told me about the picnic spots on top of the mountain, back of the University. Apparently they used to go up there quite a lot; they had special places they were fond of, and their picnics used to run to four and five hours of dining and relaxing in the sunshine, in one or other of the groves and recesses in the mountain woods.

For many years, the University property bordering on the south side of Maplewood was pretty heavily wooded all the way from Louis-Colin to Bellingham, half to three-quarters of a mile. From Maplewood the ground slopes sharply upwards; it's really the north side of the mountain. You could walk up through these woods and see a surprising amount of minor wildlife, rabbits, woodchucks, the occasional badger and plenty of game birds, pheasants and partridge, usually in pairs. Once my daughter planted some flowers and a little lettuce in the borders round our building. When the lettuce came up, rabbits from across the street ate it. I know this for a fact because I came home late one summer night and saw one of them back on his haunches on the lawn, getting into the lettuce with his forepaws. When I stopped to look at him, he took off across Maplewood and into the brush at about fifty miles per hour.

For one building project or another, the University has started to whittle away at the woods, and in five years there likely won't be anything left along the street. Up above though, especially towards Bellingham, there's still plenty of cover. There, leading down from the high point of the north side of the mountain, is the University ski run, a short but steep practice run which is quite a test of skill. There's a tow and a jump, and a downhill run beside the jump. At the bottom of the run are soccer and football fields, and the new hockey and football stadium, an ingenious and beautiful building. West and south from here are the tennis courts, set economically and sensibly into the side of the mountain, among rocky cliffs which form neither a canyon nor a gully but something in between. The steepest drop from those rock walls might be a sheer seventy-five feet, enough to give you quite a jar. All through the spring-time into June, these rocks are washed by icy water coming down from the mountainside. I'm not sure that this is just melting snow. I tasted it once and it seemed like rock-spring water to me, with a bracing mineral tang to it, very very cold.

From this sporting area, a five-minute climb takes you into a superb picnic grounds hardly touched by the University's clearances, and in the early summer a place of fantastic and unexpected beauty. You approach it from the west side of the tennis courts, where a very well-worn path leads up around the rocky cliffs through fairly heavy foliage and undergrowth, not forest but very pretty woods. The cliffs are on your left, the climb is steep, the paths diverge but the one to take is that leading around the edge of the rocks to their highest point. There is no abrupt drop here; you could climb around on the rocks if you wanted to. Lots of students and neighbourhood children do so. You might even be able to get down the sheer face of the last seventy-five feet, if you knew it well. I've never tried.

At the top of this canyon or gully (there should be a middle-sized word), you are maybe two hundred feet above the tennis courts, looking almost straight down on them. Here the woods open out a little and there are small carpets of silky, fine grass, exactly right for picnicking, mildly warm and dry, uninfested by insects, surrounded in the early summer by profusions of trilliums and other wildflowers. After M. Bourbonnais directed me to this spot, I used to spend many summer afternoons alone up there. I'd bring a loaf of French bread, some cheese, a bottle of the RAQ red Burgundy and a book, and spend the afternoon half asleep in the sun. On very clear still days, you could hear the individual words of the tennis players two hundred feet below, and sometimes a dreamily courting couple would stroll obliviously past. One such pair once fell over me before any of us were aware of each other, I full of Burgundy and sun, the boy and girl full of love.

'Je regrette, Monsieur.'

'Je vous en prie, Mademoiselle, Monsieur.'

We all laughed immoderately at the incident, then after begging my pardon again they disappeared along a path leading up past the ski jump to the very top of the mountain, another three to four hundred feet. As the sun moved the colours changed and the shadow of the thick foliage began to fall across the pages of my book; when it obscured them completely it was time to go.

On Saturdays I often found the Bourbonnais there. Monsieur and Madame, their sons, and two lovely girls, friends of the boys. They went in for very elaborate picnics lasting a long time and apparently including a huge meal and a lot of wine. When we met, they would always press a glass on me and a slice of cold chicken, with much exchange of formal politenesses on each side.

'A votre santé, Monsieur.'

'Salut, Mesdames, salut, Messieurs.'

'Encore un coup?'

'Ah oui, merci infiniment.'

After a couple of years of such pleasures we moved away. I felt sorry to say goodbye to the Bourbonnais, especially since Monsieur had not been well during our last few months in the building. He began to stay home from work, at first a day at a time, then for longer periods. There didn't seem to be anything visibly wrong with him, and I was reluctant to ask him about it. It was very unlike him to miss work, and at that when he stayed home he kept busy around the garage.

'I was there twenty-three years,' he said to me one day when I got out of my car.

'You're still there, aren't you?'

'Yes, I'll be back soon. I meant twenty-three years till now.' He kept his hands busy tying bundles in string and his eyes moved uncertainly. He seemed bewildered by what was happening to him.

'What do you do in the packing plant?'

'I'm a shipper. The man that owns this building is my boss. I load sacks of bone-meal, hundred pounds a sack. I often do that all day.'

'Sounds like heavy work.'

'It's heavy, you bet. I'm there twenty-three years and now I'm making a little over fifty a week. Fifty-two, fifty-three, take-home pay. It's not too much.'

'No.'

'No. I never missed any time before, couldn't afford it you know, with the boys in school. Now I find I'm nervous a lot.'

'You don't look nervous.' He certainly had no neurotic characteristics of any kind.

'The doctor says it's my blood-pressure, but he's not sure. It's hard, you know. He says, "Take some time off." But a man like me loses money if he takes time off; that makes things worse. Now the boys are grown up it should be easier for us, and now this.'

'Why don't you just relax and sit in a chair, instead of working around in here?'

'I can't do it. I don't know why.'

He finished the parcel he was tying, put it aside and drew me after him towards the end of the garage where his car was parked. From some dark recess in the wall, he pulled out a bag of body-worker's tools, some ball-headed hammers, tubes of filler and so on, and pointed out a dent in his right rear fender about the size of somebody's head-light.

'That's the first one. I don't count scratches. Somebody hit me in the parking lot, and he don't say a word.'

'They don't know how to park, these guys,' I said with a

good deal of bitterness. 'When they try to angle park, they hit you with the left front, isn't that it?'

He lay down under the car and began to tap softly on the body metal with a light hammer, using a rhythmic drummer's stroke. 'I think I can get it out,' he said, 'I don't want to put a hole in her, on account of the salt. I got to finish it today.'

'Why?'

He stopped hammering and put his head out from under. 'I worry about it all the time, but I can make it like new. You'll see.'

The next night when I came in he was finishing the repaint, and it matched perfectly; you'd never have guessed the dent was there. He was just blending in the repainted patch with the rest of the fender when I parked and came over to see how it looked.

'Like new,' I said.

'It's better than new. I took her right down to the bare metal, sized it, rust-proofed her and gave it five, six, coats. Better finish than the rest of the body. When I get some wax on, she'll be perfect.'

'I guess that's what you were after, eh?'

He stopped his smooth deft brush-stroke to turn and stare at me. 'I want it perfect,' he said. Under the glare of the bare light-bulb hooked to the overhead beam, his face looked leaner than ever.

I said, 'I hope you get what you want.'

Then we moved away and I didn't see much more of the Bourbonnais, though I used to see their car parked outside the building on my way home from work, always looking like it had just been polished. Once or twice I happened to see Mme Bourbonnais walking through the district with her coaster wagon and a pile of evening papers, and then we'd chat about our kids or about her husband, who wasn't making too much progress. They still couldn't pinpoint his illness. It seemed to me to be a case of a great endowment of vitality in danger of being expended too fast, too early in life. I don't offer this as a medical diagnosis; but it often seems to me that we are all given a certain amount of vitality to spend, so to speak, and M. Bourbonnais has been prodigal with his, spendthrift. It made me wonder if I wasn't perhaps a little miserly with my own capital, perhaps playing things too cagily, which is certainly one of the possible errors.

Better to be prodigal than miserly; it's the generous fault. M. Bourbonnais knew how to live, and if he gave too much and spent what he had too profusely, there was magnanimity, in the exact sense, in the gesture. And at that he was economical where necessary, so that he was enabled to spend freely. He was a damned good man.

Winter went by, and most of the next spring, and the last time I saw him was on Saint-Jean-Baptiste Day, late June, a big holiday. Even though I suspected that the top of the mountain would be full of knowing holidayers, I decided to put in an afternoon climbing around the woods for exercise, for the pleasure of the view and the sense of the weather, which had a qualified fineness that day, not the perfect blue sky, and yet not misty and hazy. Summer is short in Montréal, and even in late June you sometimes get a day which is autumnal in tone, where the colour of the sky seems to bring out soft browns and dark reds from the crowded trunks and branches in the woods. You might call it the autumn of summer's first pulse, because there is a distinct break in our summer; a few weeks from May to early July are capable of almost tropical perfection, rich greens, right in the centre of the palette, and exact blues. But later on, as you get down past mid-July, the grass and foliage start to go yellow, the sky is less and less often that glorious spring-like blue; you can get a lot of rain in August.

This particular holiday was full of presagings of the end of the perfect part of summer, the first rush of wonderful weather; there was a solemn stillness about it, and there weren't quite as many merry-makers up there as I'd feared. It was very pleasurable to slide along the narrow paths, quiet as some Indian might have been hundreds of years ago. The foliage was at its thickest and most lush, the air still and warm, lovers and picnickers content to celebrate calmly.

Suddenly I came into a little clearing at the edge of the rocks, one of my favourite places, and there were the Bourbonnais, the whole family including the two lovely girls, having a strangely quiet meal. The reason for their constraint was immediately clear. M. Bourbonnais had always been thin, but now he was emaciated. He must have lost twenty to twenty-five pounds from his slight frame, and his skin looked very bad, chalky, almost colourless. When I came into the clearing, he struggled to his feet and greeted me. It was strange to observe the ghost of his usual self haunting, as it were, this unrecognizable and dwindled body. In his shaky and hesitant movements, I could trace the sure-footed and energetic activity I was used to in him. He smiled slowly and proposed that I join him in a glass of wine.

I said, '*Ça me plairait, Monsieur,*' and drank with him. He coughed. His family stood sadly watching us, then they began to talk with great animation, especially Madame. I nodded and smiled at her, and answered one or two inquiries about the children; then I inclined my head questioningly towards her husband.

'He's gone back to work,' she said, 'he wanted to.' Her eyes were very bright and she opened and shut them twice. Sunlight shone on her bright head.

'I'm going for a climb,' I told them, and they all wished me a pleasant holiday, and then I continued along the path towards the piles of boulders, rubble and fill, along the side of the ski jump. Then I climbed some more till I was on the approach to the jump itself, right at the top, above lovers and picnickers. I sauntered out towards the very edge. The approach rises and the sides of the artificially constructed mound fall sharply away on either side. The view becomes staggering as you go out farther, a wide wide vision of the northern half of the city, the country beyond, and the ridge of hills, the first upthrust of the Laurentians, thirty miles north. You have the sense of the world dropping away from you.

The day wasn't sharply clear; outlines were blurred, and one's judgement of distance became confused, although the vision was good. Standing on the edge, right where a skier would push off for the quick descent to the jumping-off point, I could see the main east-west runway at Dorval twenty miles away to the west, as though it were right under my feet. It looked from where I stood as if you could step in a single stride onto the edge of the runway, or into the next world.

I could look directly down on the Bourbonnais, still soberly picnicking, and below them again on girlish tennis players whirling short skirts, a strangely mixed perspective, but I couldn't hear any voices. That old woman on University had climbed and stood waiting for her green light; the tennis players chased their ball; and Monsieur Bourbonnais wanted it perfect. They were all within their rights. Human purpose is inscrutable, but undeniable.

One Way North and South

THE PARKS, THE PARKS, no place has parks like ours in the summer; their names make a litany: Parc Jarry, Parc Beaubien, Fletcher's Field, Lac des Castors, Ile Sainte-Hélène, Coronation way out west, Rockland flat and sandy, Kent Park on Côte des Neiges with elaborate children's playground, football and baseball and soccer fields, and a fine battery of lights for night ball illuminating a dozen city blocks most nights in July and August. Kennedy Park has supervised swimming classes; in Joyce Park, expert tumblers and wrestlers instruct adolescents. Pratt Park has the duckpond where toy sailboats and ducks mingle amicably before a rapturous audience. Saint-Viateur and Stuart, Trenholme Park where they play very swift senior baseball, parks in Chomedy and Pierrefonds and Terrebonne and Rosemont. Small irregularly shaped parks with little stone bridges and deftly gardened lawns and waterfalls and flowerbeds; enormous oblong parks for sport; mountainside parks for taking a view of the life of the whole city. The Botanical Gardens. In a nameless little park Beaubien près Iberville, you can hear a free band concert while you wait in summer twilight for the second show at Le Dauphin.

Urban life is full enough of strain, God knows, and if it were not for the parks the multilingual confrontations of our two million might soon become unbearable.

Queen of Montréal parks, best-loved, most used and loveliest, most necessary safety valve, Parc Lafontaine is a life-saver, right where it's needed most, the southern boundary running along Sherbrooke east, just above that rolling lip of hill which drops down through the south centre of the city to the port. That steep descent imprisons sixty-three thousand desperately confined lives (I can quote exact figures), and if it weren't for the great park on top of the hill, along those crowded streets, one-way south, one-way north, Montcalm, Beaudry, Visitation, Panet, Plessis, there could be serious trouble here. There's trouble anyway.

Victoria Day in the middle of the park. Crowds. Not peaceful, turbulence, running and shouting. Knots of boys and young men divide, rush together, boil in vortices, then move concertedly in an angry wave towards the base of a statue. A man of twenty-five in dark red sweater and narrow-legged corduroy pants runs past, carrying a broad paint brush with bright red enamel dripping from it. Where are the customary girls? There is an awful lot of angry shouting.

'*A bas la reine d'Angleterre.*'

'*Donald Gordon à la potence.*'

'*Pas un sou à Ottawa.*'

'*Québec libre. Vive l'indépendance. Lesage le vendu.*'

At the centre of the great park is the serpentine artificial lake rimmed with concrete walk, a mile in circumference. Two small sternwheelers, models of Mississippi riverboats, ply this lake laden with men and girls and surrounded by rented skiffs. Today three skiffs float bottom upwards, oars floating off in the distance like sunlit toothpicks. The river steamers are now tied up by their proprietors for fear of mutinous and destructive marine horseplay, and a crowd of seventy or eighty stands on the dock looking at them and arguing about commandeering them for a naval demonstration. Someone is pushed into the lake amid cheers, then someone else, and it looks as if the tone of the assembly will remain fairly peaceable, although the counter girls in the restaurant stand well away from the windows. The *pissoir* downstairs is crowded with darkly threatening youths in Belmondo haircuts and pathetically smart shoes, bought on Ste-Catherine east, *aucun dépot requis, quarante semaines à payer.*

Six police cars along Amherst and along the roads inside the park. Motorcycles snarl slowly along Rachel. There are many children in the elaborate and entrancing children's zoo, whom nobody wants to frighten. Several hundred older people in the park begin to extricate themselves from the situation, by sitting stiffly and unseeingly on benches, or by getting into their cars and rolling up the windows and baking in the heat. Some go to the restaurant and nervously buy hotdogs and orange drinks. It's unthinkable that they'll be assaulted as they clutch this holiday lunch.

The open-air auditorium where operettas are staged has been closed so far this year, the gates padlocked, but the fences are low and now the stage is crowded with running cursing demonstrators, while a hundred more sit in the bleachers and encourage them.

About a quarter to three, a small European car with New York plates moves slowly into the park by way of one of the service roads. Inside are two youngish women, schoolteachers from North Pole, N. Y., who have been to Montréal fifty times before.

'Never any trouble,' they cry tearfully later on, 'never anything like this.'

A boy of fifteen sees the New York plates and hollers, 'Sacrément, maudits Yankee.' That does it. In two minutes a horde surrounds the car and boys start to beat on the closed windows while reciting untranslatable obscenities. The terrified faces of the women are pressed against the windows of their small car, and they don't know what to do, try to get out and plead with their tormentors or stay inside in comparative safety. The crowd increases and the tone of the noise grows ominous. Now they are tilting the little car; under the strain, a half-rusted-out bumper pulls away from the body.

Laughter. The women in the car are vomiting because of the airlessness, their fright, the motion, and the body metal resounds with slaps and bumps and kicks.

Here come the cops and first thing they grab a tall thin man with a leather jacket with LES CHEVALIERS DE L'INDÉPENDANCE NATIONALE on the back. More cops. The fighting starts and Gilles O'Neill, who has had hold of the loose bumper, lets it drop, scratches his hands painfully, and backs through the crowd wondering what to do. What began as a rude joke has suddenly gone wrong. He thinks, 'Enough, better go,' then quickly thinks again and moves uncertainly towards the nearest bunch of rolling heaving agitators who are having trouble with two big cops. Gilles gets to the edge of this group, somebody stomps hard on his left foot and the pain impels him forward; he grabs at the shoulders of a man in front of him, trying to pull him aside so as to get at one of the cops. The cops are Québécois and aren't too happy with what they're doing, you can see. As they go for their nightsticks, the shouts get more and more menacing.

'*Un autre samedi de la matraque!*'

'*Salauds Gestapos!*'

Part of Gilles's mind urges him forward, another part says no, get back, people will get hurt, what are you doing here? Then he hears heavy voices behind him and half turns. Somebody grabs his shoulder with crushing fingers and pulls, a motorcycle cop making his move from the rear. He tries to get Gilles in a bear-hug and this assault maddens Gilles – he hasn't done anything yet but shove, so he screams wordlessly at the cop and pulls and turns to run. A ripping noise by his shoulder.

Gilles takes a very hard blow high on the right side of his head, above and behind the ear, and his knees buckle. As he sinks he realizes that he'd better get out, but he can't run, people fall over him and he gets terribly frightened that he'll be trampled and badly hurt. He feels wet in his hair.

He opens his eyes and forces himself to stand. About two feet in front of him is a cop's face staring straight into his; the face works, the jaws open and shut, but there's too much noise to hear. It's a big red face. A hand grabs Gilles but he pulls back, the ripping noise again, he runs, just as the struggling crowd bursts open and people begin to go in all directions. He runs so he won't be taken to the station, to spend the night there and pay a fine out of his scooter money. Runs down the centre service road towards Sherbrooke with dozens of others, ducking around parked cars, jumping fences, gets to Sherbrooke Street, turns to look behind, sees another policeman coming near, darts across the street, finds himself corner Panet – and ducks down the hill away from the park towards home, six blocks south. Below the lip of the hill he feels safe, in his own country, nobody will follow him. A girl his own age seems to materialize in front of him like a ghost, a girl from parish school, grown up and very pretty, Denise Gariépy.

'What's the matter with you, you're a mess, you're all bleeding, your head, what is it?'

He puts his hand to his scalp, fingers a big lump and gets his hands sticky with blood. His hair is matted with it, and his hands are cut and bleeding from the little car's bumper. He is panting and feels sick.

'Who tore your coat?' He looks at the sleeve of his jacket, nearly parted from the shoulder, the seam torn most of the way around. There's another great tear from the pocket to the hem.

'A dirty cop. It cost twenty-nine fifty, this coat, and I just finished paying for it.' Standing in the middle of the sidewalk, he tries to get his composure back. He remembers Denise very well. She used to win medals for catechism and lived at the corner of Logan next to the grocery store; later her family moved north, out of the district, somewhere above Sherbrooke and east of the park. He says, 'There was a bit of trouble when we were demonstrating and I got in a fight. This cop grabbed me. He hit me on the head, good and hard. I was lucky to get out of it.'

She says, 'I was going home. I've been visiting the Archambaults. But I'll walk back down with you.'

She's really very pretty. 'All right. It will make me look innocent.' He takes off his jacket, bundles it over his arm and they walk off together, south on Panet. 'You think that's something,' he says boldly, 'just wait till July!'

Gilles lives in *le centre-sud* of the city, described by sociologists as a dying district with an increasingly aging and shrinking population. '*Un des quartiers les plus déshérités de la métropole.*' It's about four square miles in area, roughly rectangular, bounded by the Main and D'Iberville on the east and west, and by Sherbrooke Street and the port installations along the river. East and west the district is traversed by four main streets: Ontario, Ste-Catherine, Dorchester, and Craig, each with a distinct character. The contrast between Ste-Catherine and Dorchester, a block apart, is miraculous; the former is still a big shopping street, dying district or not, while Dorchester looks like an avenue of ghosts, bare, bare, bare, with the small residential enclaves below it obviously moribund.

Several years ago the main residential space along the south side of Dorchester as far as Craig, from Amherst to Papineau, was levelled, cleared by fire and sword so to speak, to make way for the new headquarters of CBC Montréal, an enormous television city. But the new building project got hung up on one snag after another, political, economic, and the acreage sits there empty, leaving this death-wound in the life of the neighbourhood.

There have been other clearances too, around the site of an important Métro station, and for new approaches to the Jacques-Cartier bridge, which discharged a further floating population on the remainder of *le centre-sud*. A lot of these people don't earn enough to live in any other part of town. Well over half the men living here earn under three thousand a year; fewer than a seventh (mostly doctors and lawyers) earn more than six thousand. Two percent of those eligible go to university. When Gilles O'Neill got banged on the head, in the riot in Parc Lafontaine, he was getting thirty-eight bucks a week as an apprentice motor-mechanic in the Dumouchelle Garage on DeMontigny.

While the clearances were going forward, a lot of artists scurried around the district south of Dorchester, taking likenesses of small taverns and grocery stores, unanimously in agreement that this was almost the most picturesque part of town. They got down much detailed notation of exactly why this place was so attractive, so there will be some records for the archives. But they couldn't really describe how it felt to live there, and now the feeling is almost irrecoverable. You can guess the sweetness and leisurely pace by looking at sketches and by analogy with similar, more northerly, quarters. You have to use your imagination.

Picturesque: condescending word. Should be reserved to painters for technical use. I don't consider the local life of Paroisse Saint-Jacques or Saint-Pierre Apôtre or Sainte-Brigide, what you see strolling along Lagauchetière Est around L'Hôpital de la Miséricorde in any way deprived or impoverished except in the purely economic sense, but nowadays that sense is taken to be central. Is it? In those old parishes, there was much stagnation, no doubt, and sometimes acute poverty and hunger, which is painful and undeniable. But there was something valuable too, which made the place awfully good to contemplate, not merely picturesque or quaint, but self-assured, cohesive, admirable, a social unit that really worked, before the march of progress supplanted it with an enormous vacant lot.

People had an intimate understanding of each other's affairs, their employment, their income, their beliefs. 'Everybody knew everybody else.' Dozens of small, economically indefensible grocery stores and other enterprises kept their owners alive, able to provide the centres around which many local customs could take root and flourish. There was hunger, dirt, there were bugs, but there was no problem with juvenile crime. You could walk along the darkest alley in perfect safety. There were a lot of damned good taverns and a couple of famous ones. What you saw, behind the trivially picturesque, was a populous society which provided almost all its members with qualified content-ment, and a sense of being at home in the world. 'Nobody lives like that now.' Right. Nobody does.

Some elements of this life persist, north of Dorchester, all the way up to Parc Lafontaine along the cross-streets, one way north and south: Beaudry, Visitation, Panet, where Gilles O'Neill has always lived, and where Denise Gariépy lived until she was twelve or thirteen, when her father was doing well enough to move uptown to an enormous apartment on Delorimier, and to keep Denise in school and then send her to the Université de Montréal. On these streets the mutual loyalty and cohesion of the group, and its relaxed attitude towards the individual, are expressed in the rich variety of the appearance of the houses, within a recurring pattern. Walking up Plessis from De Montigny, say, you find row housing with, every eight units, a carriage-entry leading into a courtyard surrounded by staircases, more homes. Wherever you look, the elevations are slightly different, no two are repeated. Here a big window is rimmed by an elaborately carved wooden frame; there a tiny house interrupts the row, its roof five feet lower than the others. This is a wilderness of camera-angles no film-maker has spot-ted. And Gilles's street is just the same, so is the next one over, Visitation, although there is one almost excessively individual building there, the Ecole de Boxe Reggie Chartrand; Apprenez à vous défendre, which was for several years the *siège social* of Les Chevaliers de l'Indépendance National. Now it is dark at night, and signs saying À VENDRE and À LOUER hang on the white walls alongside placards announcing that Reggie Chartrand will contest a seat in the approaching provincial elections, on a strictly *indépendantiste* platform. He must have decided that constitutional means suffice for effective social revolution, a hopeful augury.

Gilles used to hang around the Chartrand gym, after he left school at the end of tenth year, a lot later than most of his friends. For a while in his early teens he had the idea that he might be able to become an engineer; he had a natural appreciation of mechanical design. A few people from the neighbourhood had acquired advanced education, usually the sons of professional men. It was almost unheard of for a girl to go as far as university, which is why everybody knew of Denise Gariépy, even though she'd moved away four or five years ago. Her father sold fuel oil and heating equipment (a profitable line of goods in our climate) and had done a hell of a lot better than he ever expected. He hadn't much education and intended to see that his children would do even better than he had. Denise was the first girl in the family to go to university, where she was preparing a *licence* in the *faculté des lettres*. When she had her degree in history, she would go into government or teaching.

So Gilles knew all about her when he met her on Victoria Day, the remarkable girl, sometimes discussed as an example of *l'épanouissement des nôtres* by sober old men and ladies in fairly good circumstances, rue Panet. She was pretty hard on Gilles as they walked towards his home.

'You are fools, you are babies. How old are you?'

'The same as you, maybe a year older. We were in the same class.'

'Nineteen?'

'I'll be twenty soon.'

'And you've nothing better to do than shout in the park with the rest of them? You'll get nowhere doing that.'

'What else is there to do? I don't have a car. I'm saving to buy a scooter, and it'll take another two years.'

'What do you do?'

'I work for Dumouchelle.'

'Old Dumouchelle won't pay you enough to buy a scooter. I thought you were going to stay in school.'

'Not enough money.'

'That's foolish. You'll never make any money where you are now.'

This tone of moral superiority annoyed him, and the cuts in his hands were hurting. The whole afternoon seemed like a stupid waste of time. When they came to his home, just below Logan, he said, 'How will you get home from here? If I had my scooter I could take you.'

'I don't mind walking.'

'Will you go for a walk with me? Sometime soon?'

'Yes. But I won't come in the park to watch you fight.'

'We'll find something else to do.' She smiled and walked away north, and Gilles went inside and washed his hands. Hot water, he found, hurt them very much.

After that they saw each other often. In the evenings through June and early July, he would walk east on Ontario Street to Delorimier, where he would pause for a minute or two to stare at the ancient deserted baseball stadium, once the home of the Montréal Royals, and later a rollerdrome and the home of a fugitive professional football team, and now at the end of its useful life. In the old days this corner would be jammed with activity on a Sunday afternoon, half a dozen policemen directing traffic and thousands filing into the ball park. Gilles, born the year Jackie Robinson played with the Royals, was too young to feel any nostalgia about baseball, but he could remember being taken for walks by his father, along Ontario Street in the midst of hurrying excited crowds, and he had shared their excitement.

Standing on the dark corner on summer evenings, he felt puzzled about his life and his future, which seemed a dead end. What could he do? His pay was inching up. In six or seven years, he might earn eighty dollars a week, perhaps more, but never enough to save anything and get anywhere. He acted mighty thoughtful those nights; when he turned away from the deserted stadium, it was as if leaving ghostly thousands cheering behind him as he walked north, up the steep hill on Delorimier.

Up the hill and across Sherbrooke, things changed, he could

feel the change. It was like climbing out of a pit – you could smell possibilities in the air – there are no major barriers north along Delorimier. From here a man might move anywhere, to Rosemont, to Montée Saint-Léonard, an easy transition. Delorimier north of Sherbrooke is darkly mysterious and inviting from twilight forwards, about the longest day in the year.

The street is lined on either side by great oaks and maples, and behind them those massive dwellings of the recurring Montréal type, six to eight large homes in each building. They are imposing and solid, but it isn't the buildings that compose the effect; it's the trees. In late June twilight, there will still be some light in the sky at nine-thirty, in the western segment, from the recent sun. This great flood of light seems to move, as you come north along the street, rolling over the edge of the skyline formed by the houses and spreading like liquid through the crowding branches of the trees. It's a strange colour, a light silvery purple, very smooth and even, and it deepens from moment to moment. When there is a breeze, as is usual in this city, the trees are full of a soft rushing breathy sound. And if you turn suddenly on your heel and look south over the edge of the hill, your gaze leaps the *centre-sud*, hidden from view by the drop of the hill, straight to the enormous Jacques-Cartier bridge, looking like a tremendous dalmatic of black and gold hung over the river, sparkling, alive, headlights.

Leaves sighed, turned, stillness, a soft rush of breeze, then stronger, hushed voices from balconies, now a sharp break of laughter and the clink of glasses, then children objecting to their bedtime. Along came Gilles to the staircase where Denise waited for him; they would walk and argue quietly for hours.

'Le silo sans graine,' he said, the night after Saint-Jean-Baptiste. They had watched the *défilé* the night before and their feet were tired.

She laughed. 'Where did you hear that?'

It was an obscene reference to the women's residence at the university.

'Everybody knows about it,' he said, rather sulkily.

'But I don't live there. I couldn't afford it and I wouldn't want to. I like it here.'

'You've got a nice big home. I wish your father liked me.'

'He does, but he thinks you have no future.'

'He's right.'

'He got away, and he had nothing to start with. You could be an engineer or a technician; he had nothing like that. You could do just as well.'

'What has he done?'

'He got us a good place to live, and sent us to school. Are you perfectly contented? What did you mean when you said "Wait till July"?'

'When did I say that?'

'That day I met you, when you'd been fighting.' She was quiet for a moment and then said, 'You seemed ... stupidly heroic. The real student leaders, the boys in *sciences sociales, lettres,* they don't riot in the park. They do something to get what they want. I don't say they aren't revolutionaries, because the best of them are. But they'll direct the revolution. And all you can do is what you're told.'

'A stupid hero?'

'*Un petit soldat.*'

Gilles missed the reference. 'I'm twenty. I can't go back to school, and anyway there isn't any place for me to go to school, a free school.'

'If you don't go back to school, you're ruined for life. In six months you could get your eleventh year.' Then she was silent, wouldn't say any more that evening, walked quietly beside him to her staircase, kissed him fervently for half an hour and sent him home to figure it out.

Gilles thought; stupid hero, that's part good and part bad, and it isn't a sin to be stupid, just bad luck. That means she likes me very much. She knew what I meant by 'Wait till July'.

He had intended to get involved in a really stupid, misdirected and surprisingly destructive demonstration which took place on Canada Day, but his meditations kept him out of it; he thought she wouldn't like it, perhaps with reason. What would the eleventh year cost him, could he get it for nothing during his free hours, or would he have to spend his scooter money, and a lot more too?

In the bad old days in this province, the eleventh year wouldn't get you into university, and unless you wanted to be a poorly paid teacher there were few institutions granting anything after the eleventh year apart from a few certificates of half-skilled technical aptitude. Gilles didn't want to be a *garagiste* till he died, but until this year he'd have been blocked off from higher education, even if he had his eleventh year. Now, in an age of educational revolution, it was just starting to seem possible that people like him, hitherto forgotten by educators, might be able to salvage their talents and intelligence and ambition. There was a race going on between the educational reformers and the violently revolutionary impulse of the neglected and suppressed.

Denise knew all about this, all about the most significant reform of the province's system, the foundation of *les instituts* which were to link secondary school and the first university year, which would offer both liberal and technical options, which would be free, offering the twelfth to fourteenth years of education to all who had standing in the eleventh. Gilles might be able to arrive at *le niveau universitaire* if he had that eleventh, instead of being condemned to mental degradation and rioting in the park, aimless, self-destructive, vicious.

In two years she would become an *institutrice* in one of these new schools, and later on perhaps a department head. She could see the potential effects of legislated reform, and how exactly the race between stability and explosion was displayed in Gilles. If he could suffer obscurity and indignity just a little bit longer, put up with it and control himself, his intelligence and her love could take him through his fourteenth year and into the university. He could be an engineer at twenty-seven instead of a qualified mechanic, and his prospects would, she considered, open and improve, and grow liberal.

She kept after him. 'You can get the eleventh year at night. I'll help you. I'll even teach you.' When he grimaced, she had her answer ready. 'It's no disgrace to let a girl help you. If you finish next spring, you can start in an institute as soon as it opens.'

'When would that be?'

'September, a year from now.'

Like an awful lot of Montréalers, he had been waiting a long time for something like this, and he was sceptical. 'How do you know for sure?'

'I'll be almost ready to teach in one.'

They had walked west along Rachel and now came abreast of the park. Some distance to their left, and a little behind them, a baseball game was being played under lights and the shouts of the crowd were carried to them, now faint, now cheerfully loud. Towards the lake it was quieter, and down a slope at the edge of the water it was tranquil. They strolled along the edge of the lake, paused, and stood looking at the dark calm water and the reflections of the stars.

'You weren't here, *le premier juillet?*'

'I stayed away because of you.'

'I'm good for you.' She was very small girl, lightly built but round, with enormous eyes, an appealing combination. She wasn't in the habit of ordering men about. 'I only ask for this because I love you,' she said.

'How still it is tonight,' he said, feeling sober and mature. Then he laughed and took a passionate decision, which mixed startlingly with their embrace. He could smell her perfume and thought, *'Drôle d'institutrice.'* 'I'll do it. I couldn't do it for anyone else, but I'll wait some more. I'll study and I'll wait.' The park was still; he was aroused by a dozen emotions and held her as tightly as he could. 'I'll wait a year, but you'll have to keep your promise.'

Poor little Denise Gariépy, kissed and caressed by a people's whole history. She felt the strain. She said, 'Wait, you'll see … wait,' and stretched out beside him on the lakeside bank.

The Village Inside

FROM SAINTE-ANNE-DE-BELLEVUE to Pointe-aux-Trembles is thirty-five miles – which sounds like the refrain to a folk song:

> In summer on this island
> God's sweet sun smiles.
> From Sainte-Anne to the Point
> 'Tis thirty-five miles.

And from the port to the back river, at the widest span, is fifteen miles. These distances may not be precise to the foot, but it's a big island, a lot bigger than, say, Manhattan, and therefore with plenty of open space between the dozens of municipalities dotting the countryside: Sainte-Anne-de-Bellevue, Pointe-Claire, Dorval, Pierrefonds, Dollard des Ormeaux, Saraguay, Ville Saint-Laurent. These place-names are like musical notes in a rich orchestration, each with a history and mythology and traditions.

In summer I do a lot of bicycling, the best way to explore the outer reaches of the island, because of the fair weather and the distances involved. In an afternoon or evening's ride, you can get over twenty miles out and twenty back. Starting from the centre of town, where I live, you can't quite get off the island, east or west, and back again, between lunchtime and dinner, or between dinner and the eleven o'clock news – that's a bit too far, unless you were foolhardy enough to bicycle along one of the main highways, the Metropolitan or Number Two, or Côte de Liesse, which would be courting instant death.

Sticking to back roads and the main streets of suburbs, twenty miles out and back is plenty, and will take you almost anywhere you might wish to go, to investigate and see how the city has remorselessly enveloped the identity of one village after another, often without the formality of political union, an oversight which now causes endless trouble in the management of essential services, the smaller towns retaining their formal independence with great jealousy. Sooner or later we'll probably come to some sort of borough government. Already the towns on Ile Jésus, to the north, have agglomerated, and the provincial authorities and the city council are urging further steps in the process.

Cries of 'They'll never take us alive!' from Westmount, Outremont, the Town of Mount Royal and other places.

And at that they have a point, especially the more distant communities, because it isn't long since most of them existed quite independently of the city, and naturally they have local institutions and customs, and powers, that they mean to safeguard. In the thirties, before the Metropolitan and the Trans-Canada were built, a small town ten miles from the centre of the city – even though in full view of the dome of the Oratory – might enjoy a somnolent nineteenth-century style of life, without excessive gasoline fumes and traffic, without shopping centres and intimidating prairies of blacktop, without every modern inconvenience, because such a place could only be reached with some difficulty on narrow local roads.

Just this side of Terrebonne, east along the back river, there used to be, and perhaps still is, a bridge so narrow and frail that automobile traffic was only permitted one way at a time; there was an ingenious traffic light at either end which allowed cars to proceed south for a short time, then reversed itself and let people come the other way. Not too many people took that route to Terrebonne without good reason. Now that this rickety anachronism has been superseded by a four-lane concrete structure a few miles west (a genuine advance, I'm not knocking it for a minute), Terrebonne is bigger, noisier, richer, and fully into the twentieth century.

Sometimes the overlay of city on remote village can be traced, building by building, along an old main street. In August, ranging wider and wider on my bike in the evenings, trying to crowd in all the sunshine coming to me before autumn, I discovered rue Sainte-Croix out in Saint-Laurent, not really remote, simply the continuation of Lucerne after it passes under the elevated highway. True enough, it's no more than five miles from the centre of town, but you can detect the ancient village inside the suburban growth, like an attenuated ghost, traceable by houses spotted along the street as you ride north, interrupted by modern installations of a qualified beauty and utility.

Coming north from the Metropolitan, you ride first of all along a characterless strip of land – to your right a modern burial park without any headstones. I once went to a funeral there, stepped out of a limousine onto a flat recessed plaque of debased design, and remarked to the widow without thinking that it was the kind of place where you didn't know who you might be walking on. I really didn't mean to upset her.

On the left are various industrial buildings rimming the highway service roads, and then, between these and the memorial park, the traffic is funnelled towards a highly inconvenient railway crossing, always jammed with heavy trucks. Once across the tracks, you see on your right the first of a long chain of enormous ecclesiastical and collegiate buildings, the oldest dating perhaps from the late eighties, all belonging in one way or another to the administration of the Collège de Saint-Laurent, the principal educational institution in the town. There are various classroom and residence buildings and a great church, and off behind the campus the Saint-Laurent arena with attached sports facilities, a shooting gallery, gymnasium, and so on, apparently run by the college.

Juste en face on the left side of Sainte-Croix going north, there begins to appear the ghostly presence of the old town, which must have dozed peacefully in the August sun, remote from all urban troublings of the heart, at least until the mid-forties, to judge by the age of the buildings. Between rue du Collège and rue de l'Eglise, facing the expanse of institutional lawns and flower-beds, are five or six small wooden buildings of unexampled beauty, two of them abandoned or to let, the others perverted from their original purposes to rather mean uses, as coalsheds or small offices for industrial storage lots. One of these buildings must have been a group of three dwellings, row houses, a storey and a half in height, with low mansard roof. A sagging verandah stretches the short length of the row, and the entries (two of them boarded over) are of great delicacy.

Further up the street there's a superb stone farmhouse of the kind you still see all over the richer farmland of western

Québec, two storeys and an attic, of immensely solid irregular stones, maybe a hundred and twenty years old and now the offices of a small local construction company. Further along there's a Victorian mansion with a tower surrounded by balconies, red brick with a pattern of darker, almost bluish, stone let into the wall. Who can have lived there? An early mayor, the richest man in the village? Houses like these, about ten of them set among gas stations and gravel yards, suggest the tidal-wave movement of an enormous city's advance in every direction, like debris surfacing from a sunken wreck.

Sainte-Croix isn't the main street of Ville Saint-Laurent any more; west a few blocks we find the northern stretches of Decarie, and west again from that the truly modern street, Boulevard Laurentien, a four-lane divided highway running north off the island. Here are the offices of Canadair and the eastern border of Cartierville airport, haven for light planes and local airways. On the other side of the local airport, five or six miles west and south, is Dorval International, one of the busiest airports on the continent, jets coming onto the east-west runways almost every minute round the clock.

It's an eerie sight, standing on rue Sainte-Croix, in front of the evident ghost of a nineteenth-century Québec village, to see overhead jet after jet slanting down and in towards the Dorval runways, almost without intervals between arrivals. You have the impression of one time superimposed on another, with both visibly present, something quite rare.

Boulevard Laurentien is all tremendous breadth and modernity and speed, with light planes of every size parked in dense ranks on the west side, and vast infinities of blacktop – a Dali horizon – on the east, supermarkets and shopping centres shrunk into distant insignificance by the grandeur of the black space around them, with its beautiful and complex pattern of yellow parking marking. Off to the north and east are housing developments, their tone just opposite to that of rue Sainte-Croix. And nevertheless, oddity of oddities, these opposed patterns merge at one special point, in an extraordinarily graphic way.

There must have been outlying farms stippled around the village a few hundred yards apart. On one amazing corner, now, this year, you come past a mile of blacktop – the shopping centre can scarcely be seen in the distance because of the glare – and suddenly you see a hundred-and-forty-year-old wooden farmhouse standing on a fifty-by-fifty plot of land, on the extreme corner of the titanic parking lot, ready to fall off the edge into history. It's a magnificent house. It seems incomparably more lonely in its present situation, under the perpetual jets, than it could have in 1867 when the night lights of other farms could scarcely be distinguished.

The front door faces south, away from the prevailing winds; there is no garage nor any room to park a car on the property, no TV aerial. A pump stands at the back of the house, black-green, unused perhaps for fifty years. I know there's electricity because one room – never more than one – is lit at night.

I often bicycled past this place in the early August evenings, drawn to the site to admire the way the soft grained sheen of the walls took the light just after sunset. Once, I recall, there was a sensational display of sunset colour of the kind that entices bad painters, a whole western skyful of grey and rose tones that you might perhaps see in nature once in ten years, but which you'd be crazy to put in a painting – nobody would believe it. As I stood across the street from the farmhouse, the colours reflected on its western wall began to deepen; night was coming on and overhead immense airplane after airplane drew down over me, roaring, landing-gear already out, lights at wingtips. There was a stiff breeze blowing from the north down the highway. Rose tones darkened and were merged in deep blue; all at once it was night. In the house the single light came on, downstairs in what was probably the living room. For some reason my curiosity about the people in the house became intense, and spotting a hamburger shack two blocks south I went and had a coffee, and made the inquiries which elicited this story.

Victor Latourelle, a farmer born in the nineties, had always lived in the house. When he was born, this was full, deep countryside, no highways, no cars, for all practical purposes no city, no Oratory, no university tower, at nights nothing in the sky but the moon and stars. On the back river, serious and unpolluted fishing and hunting. The Latourelle family owned seventy acres, blissfully ignorant of the potential value of the land; they got their living from it, that was all. They had always done so, or so it must have seemed because at that time the house was already close to seventy years old.

Victor Latourelle must have crept across stubbly fields to dirt tracks into the village, so as to attend parish school for a few years, with here and there a barn lifting on his horizon, and in the village the raw new collegiate buildings, ambitious and out-sized, which we find there still. At twenty he was left untouched by the *crise de conscription*; he didn't recognize its existence. He helped work the farm and lived as he'd always done, and nobody bothered him.

Perhaps in the nineteen-twenties, when automobiles made their way more regularly along those outlying country roads, the accelerating pace of social change may now and then have impressed him faintly. Some crazy biplane, alone in the sky, may have impelled him to point it out and laugh. Here an occasional rudimentary gasoline pump, there (very distant) a minor industrial installation. His children began to grow up; there were only three of them (to rebut the myth of the large French-Canadian family), a daughter and two sons, all born in the decade between 1915 and 1925. The daughter, Victorine, the youngest, was always his favourite, and after modern life began to touch the Latourelle farm, to some degree his cross.

After the second war, the signs of the impending destruction of the traditional Latourelle family life were evident, pressing, impossible to ignore. The boys had never lived on the farm, the first generation in the family to live and work in the city. But Victorine married a local boy who came to live on the place, ostensibly to assist in its operation. Their wedding took place in 1947, and in a year or two they began to agitate for the sale of the land, as was perhaps only natural in their position. In the next twenty years, the property regularly appreciated in value, enough by 1965 to enrich the family, and more particularly Victorine and her husband, André Savard.

Consider M. Latourelle's position. He had never lived any-where else, and didn't want to. He was into his late fifties and might very comfortably live out his time where he'd been born, leaving the farm to be disposed of after his death however the children might decide. He had no false romantic ideas about the place, no semi-mystical commitment to the land such as we read about in novels. He just hoped to stay put. He knew that the boys, and his grandchildren, had abandoned his kind of life forever, that sooner or later his home would be swallowed up. He simply didn't want to be the one to take the final step.

Now a seventy-acre farm is just barely viable, if that, in today's market. Victor could see that as soon as the first little slice was taken off his land, the rest would inevitably follow. He fought very hard against family pressure, especially from M. and Mme Savard, right there in the house with him; but after nearly ten years of constant cajolery from Victorine, whom he loved, he sold off a ten-acre strip at the east of his place to some real-estate developers (perfectly honest and fair-dealing men, as it happened) who ran a road along it, threw up something they called Airview Park, and made a pile of dough from what was actually a pretty small project. Ten years after that, which brings us up almost to yesterday, that ten acres is assessed at a figure which bears no relation whatsoever to what M. Latourelle got for it, to his daughter's abundant justification. When the sale question recurred, she always needled her father about his failure to get what he should have from the first sale. She would walk over to the edge of Airview Park, in the late 1950s, and stand there sadly for an hour, wondering what the development was worth in the aggregate, at present prices. After sadness came anger and reproach.

'Next time, *pépère*, at least let us do the bargaining. It's always the same story with you, letting people take advantage of you. You could have got three times as much for that land. More. Let André handle it next time.'

Her father said mildly, 'Perhaps there won't be another time.'

'Of course, there will. There are real-estate men buzzing around here like flies. André was talking to one this morning. Crooked? He'd take the place from you for nothing if he could.'

'Then I won't sell. Time for that afterwards.' He meant after he was dead, which was not lost on Victorine; she didn't want to wait that long. She hoped to ride the booming real-estate market right to the top of the wave, and then hop off to the enrichment of the whole family. There was never any intention in her mind of cheating her brothers, or doing her father an injustice; she was in effect the voice of progress. She thought they ought to wait a certain length of time, but not till her father died, that would be too long. He was in excellent health and came of a long-lived stock; by then she'd be too old to enjoy herself. She was thirty-five, she remembered, and she put more and more pressure on her father.

'Don't sell yet, but soon, soon.' This was in the early sixties, at the top of the market, when every other stretch of land in town had been dealt off years before, when in fact the municipal council was eager to complete the development of all former farms, pushing through new streets, laying sewers and completing power circuits. Nobody in town wanted the sixty-acre Latourelle farm to remain undeveloped much longer, neither the real-estate men, nor council, nor the family.

In 1962, accordingly, M. Latourelle had to take another step in his strategic retreat, selling off an L-shaped thirty acres on the north and east sides of the farm for a very handsome figure, but not quite what Victorine would have asked. She consulted her husband at length, and her brothers' families, and they vowed that the next and last deal would be handled by the younger generation, no longer quite so young. She was bored with the old house now, especially when she shopped the new places going up all around: shower doors that rolled silently back and forth, with frosted glass and designs of fish and other marine subjects, chic bathroom wallpapers in floral or heraldic motifs, bathtubs in unusual, Pompeian shapes, diamonds or circles, his-and-hers washbasins. And the kitchens, and the closet space, and the two-car garages. She and André wanted to buy further north, towards the back river and certain new shopping and entertainment facilities. Their share of the final sale would set them up permanently in such a home.

Here the affair turned nasty, as it sometimes does. When her father decided to hang on to the last of the property till he died, she began to insinuate that he'd lost his mental competence, and that he shouldn't be allowed to stand in the way of progress. She took this argument to the council first of all. Her father was incompetent to handle his affairs and ought to be compelled to surrender his authority to his children.

'What can we do?'

'Can't you take legal action against him? Can't you expropriate or rezone the district?'

'Madame, we might rezone to allow industrial development, or apartment construction. We don't rezone to exclude or disallow a single-family dwelling on twenty-five acres. Your father is within his rights and can hold out as long as he likes.'

'Aren't you interested in the future of the town?'

'Certainly, Madame, but we can't force a property owner to sell disadvantageously. We have the legal right to insist on installing necessary services, and your father has never tried to stop us. When we put in the sewers and power lines, he was glad to have it done. He said it would make the property more valuable for you. Aren't you being a little unjust?'

'But think how it looks, that big square of stubble in the middle of the city. It looks ridiculous and ugly. He isn't farming it any more, and he's let the outbuildings fall to pieces. It's an eyesore, and you should do something about it.' She felt frantic that even the government wouldn't back her up. 'It's your duty to expropriate.'

'On the contrary, it's our duty to preserve an open real-estate market, so that your father – and you – can get the best price for your holdings. If the owner doesn't want to sell, for whatever reasons, it would be quite wrong for us to force him, unless for a major public work, and we have nothing planned for that district.'

'What about the shopping centre? Don't you want it?'

Here Mme Savard approached spongy ground. Certainly the council wanted the shopping centre, *in abstractio*, so to speak, *sub specie aeternitatis*, in the same way that every North American, English, French, Spanish, Eskimo, seems to be convinced that a new shopping centre, preferably of the largest conceivable scope, given local topography, is an inevitable harbinger of economic *épanouissement*. But a shopping centre, or plaza, to use the more modish term, is a commercial venture for private profit, and municipal officials everywhere, while normally ready to abet their construction, are chary of being identified with the interest of private developers, for the obvious legal and ethical reasons. Nobody in council was going to twist Victor Latourelle's arm to make him sell to a commercial developer. That sort of move can make you look very bad at an election, or in front of a board of inquiry from the Department of Municipal Affairs.

Mme Savard then took the more extreme step of trying to have her father certified as incompetent by a psychiatrist, with the aim of committing him to an institution for the aged. Here again she failed because her father, though by now seventy years old, was plainly excessively sane, if that's possible, so much so that not even the most unscrupulous practitioner would commit him for fear of detection by some meddlesome public authority.

After Victorine started to invite psychiatrists to the house, poor M. Latourelle caved in emotionally. 'Have I deserved this?'

'What, Papa?'

'I'm saner than you, Victorine.'

'Then sell!'

He broke down at her insistence, and an arrangement was quickly made which gave the remainder of the property, except for the fifty-foot square the house actually stood on, to the development corporation. They were not entirely happy to have the southwest corner of the parking lot encumbered by a decrepit vestige of the past. But M. Latourelle was past seventy, obviously failing, so the house would surely be available for demolition within a reasonable time.

That's how matters rest. Victorine and André took their share of the money and bought a split-level ranch with copper plumbing, up near Boulevard Gouin. Victor Latourelle lives alone, leaves his home only to buy food or visit the bank, lights a lamp in whichever room he sits alone in through the oncoming dark. Sometimes he looks out of his windows at the asphalt seas surrounding him and sees cattle grazing, his father working in their thick green truck garden, his uncle Antoine bent in a distant cornfield. Hallucinatory no doubt, but you can't really blame him.

A Green Child

THIERRY DESAUTELS, *un vrai jusqu'auboutist*, sat at the back of a 95 bus going east on Bélanger to the loop at the end of the line, about half-past ten one Thursday night in mid-September. The appliance store on Masson where he specialized in TV sales had been open till nine; he had been on his feet for twelve hours and felt light-headed, almost dazed with fatigue. He hoped he hadn't made any mistakes calculating the payments on the sale he'd made just as the store was closing. It had taken him half an hour to work out the contract for the buyer, and he had pushed him out the door with relief, quite a while after closing.

He didn't get his meals at his uncle and aunt's place on Boulevard Lacordaire, at the extreme verge of the city, so he'd eaten downtown and then caught a bus for his long ride home. It was misty, raining but still not cold, and he had his head half cradled on his arm and shoulder against the partly opened window; he drowsed, listening to the singing of tires on the wet black pavement. Sometimes the lights in the bus went momentarily dim, maybe because of a sudden drain on the electrical system, and every so often it jounced to a stop, hissed and puffed as the doors opened and shut. Then the roar and whir of the big engine, the lurch forward, and the bus continued eastwards.

Past Pie-IX, past 23rd Avenue, 25th Avenue, 27th, 31st, 33rd, past Viau, farther and farther east, and half asleep as he was, and tired and dazed, he began to sense darkness deepening at his cheek. Across Bélanger on his left the houses grew fewer and fewer, an occasional vacant lot separating straggling buildings, then another, then extended dark and empty spaces, sometimes with a sign A VENDRE stuck in the mud, wider spaces, fewer buildings – they were coming towards the end of the line and he almost let himself fall asleep; the bus driver knew him and would wake him at the last stop. Sounds merged, distinguished themselves: the sucking noise of the big windshield wipers, the thinning and declining murmur of other passengers. As the city tailed off into vacancy he began to hear the sound of the wind and the almost inaudible rain.

He remembered or dreamed or imagined the good month he was having in sales, and heard the store owner compliment him again, as he had twice in the last week, on his ability to close the sale and get the signed contracts. He would make good commissions this month. Soon he would start looking for a more comfortable place to live, closer to work, a little more space. He was fond of his aunt and uncle, who always offered him coffee and a piece of cake when he came home late; they treated him kindly and didn't pry into his affairs. He had no affairs, lived alone, worked hard, saved his money.

His head sank lower on his arm. As the bus drew near the terminus it grew almost empty. Almost the last to leave were two laughing housewives, each loaded down with an evening's shopping, who left the bus at Assomption. The driver, who had an extraordinarily narrow head and a pencil-line moustache, turned and watched them down the steps, saying good-night to them as the doors shut. The driver seemed tired too, and in no hurry to finish this leg of his run. He dug in his shirt pocket and got out his cigarettes but didn't light one, deferring the pleasure until he looped around to the parking lot at the end of the line.

Lines of lights in darkness dotted the north side of the street; it grew open and cool and almost pastoral on that side, while to the south the lines of squat new brick buildings continued, a vaguely schizoid circumstance that had deeply impressed itself on Thierry's imagination. Now there was a smooth and even breeze on his cheek, through the window from the north. The bus driver sang quietly: 'You are the one for me, for me, for-mi, for-mi-dable.'

A stippled edge of rain flipped along his cheek, waking Thierry with a bit of a jump; the store manager's voice still in his ears, praising his tact, his earning potential. He looked along the length of the bus. Only the swaying, singing driver and one other passenger were left, somebody he didn't know, which was peculiar because after eighteen months of tripping back and forth on the 95 he knew by sight almost everybody who rode at the same time as he did. The other passenger was a shining blur of reflected light, tucked in a corner of the seat by the front door. His eyes widened as he tried to dispel this illusion; then he saw that the blur of light was bouncing off the stiff, shiny folds of a transparent vinyl raincoat. He had a mixed image of waves of long dark hair, shining fabric, and a bright, waving patch of green, a scarf at the girl's throat. She didn't move and seemed unaware of his presence, and for a second he wasn't sure he was awake. Outside the Masson appliance store, shoals and schools of young women had passed and repassed the big plate glass windows all evening, the neon light rebounding from their fashionable vinyls, yellow, whorls of red and gold.

Images of trooping bands of young girls *en fleurs* merged with this present apparition, motionless, unaware of his intense stare. He shook his head to clear it, but the prevailing September mist seemed to have infiltrated the bus, and indeed his vision. He blinked, and saw more clearly that she was sitting sidewise-on, very composedly, her head turned so as to look ahead at the vast tract of blackness, the fields beyond the end of the line which now came into view. Her raincoat was narrow, clear, and she wore a dress of some middle colour underneath. What caught his eye most vividly was the bunch of green at her neck and throat, that and her lustrous hair and her immobility.

The bus stopped at the corner of Lacordaire, almost the easternmost street of all. The driver stretched his arms and sat back tiredly against his seat. The front door surged open with a puff. Thierry had a last glimpse of swinging, stiff vinyl and of dark hair. She got out and he heard her heels clack away to the corner. The rear door stuck for a moment after the green light came on and he pushed at it without concentration. Then it opened and he came along the side of the bus past the front door.

The driver lit his cigarette, drew on it, nodded familiarly and said, 'She's something new, eh?'

'Who is she?'

'She don't ride with me. I never saw her before, that I know of.'

'*Bonsoir.*'

'*... soir.*'

Thierry stared across the vacant lot at the corner to see where she'd gone, but she was out of sight remarkably quickly. The bus rolled across Lacordaire to the tail-end of the pavement at rue Valdombre, where Bélanger became a narrow muddy track winding off into obscure and uninvestigated fields; there it looped around towards the shopping centre parking lot where it came to rest, pointing west. The driver got out and finished his cigarette, then walked away into the darkness behind his vehicle which vibrated softly in neutral. Thierry turned south and went home. He rarely crossed Lacordaire – there was nothing over there – but he sometimes stared out of his window, just before going to bed, at the vast stretches of obscurity outside, broken only by the brave lights of a few new duplexes on rue D'Avila, a hundred feet of brand-new street almost buried in the darkness.

An image recurrent in the work of modern film-makers, especially in that of Antonioni, is justified in actual life by the appearance of this part of town. In *La Notte*, for example, long stretches of the beginning of the movie are devoted to images of enormous, multi-storied, unfinished structures, always in the most advanced architectural styles, growing up out of vacant lots in what was countryside a moment before, at the very edge of the huge modern city. Mastroianni and Moreau wander half-heartedly and in confusion through pitted fields, past dented oil-drums lying on their sides, under the glassy and silent walls of these gigantic and uninhabited signs of human activity. The effect is as if history were running backwards; instead of these buildings seeming the heralds of stunning development, of a new age, they seem under Antonioni's harsh inspection to be the ruined monuments of a past describable now only by archaeological investigation; they seem deserted as if by a panic-stricken populace after some fearful disaster. Scaffolding enshrouds them in silence, nobody working. Piles of rubble, eroded by impersonal winds, flow slowly downwards into unfinished parking garages which have never lodged a car. The wind moves the grass and weeds; rain falls; emptiness is reflected in new windows already dirtied and cracked. Walls are missing in odd places on top storeys; perhaps a rusting piece of construction equipment, a bulldozer or power shovel, stands hopelessly embedded in mud.
     Seen at certain times, in insufficient or misty light, the

extreme east of Montréal elicits this melancholy interpretation. Here are dozens of great new buildings, each with some striking architectural feature: one is circular in form, each storey staggered in or out, so as to provide a maximum of healthful light to the patients. Another is set cleverly on stilts, with the structural principles of the higher floors explained by the cement uprights of the ground floor. Another is in bright stripes of glazed brick, alternately green and grey, with black window frames forming a curious checkerboard up the walls. These and other similar buildings, finished and half finished, are apt to be set down in fields of solid mud, with a hundred feet of open dumping ground between them and their neighbours. And all around is emptiness and the smell of raw turned earth, and piles of ashes and eggshells. No matter how far east the buildings go there is space beyond.

The most arresting of these desert monuments is the Montée de Saint-Léonard interchange on the east-island section of the Trans-Canada highway. It is colossal, and will eventually connect a dozen traffic patterns in superb economy and efficiency of movement; no expense or effort has been spared on its design. For example, each of the great concrete uprights supporting the entry ramps, and each curving run of wall along the overpasses, has been ornamented with individual patterns of abstract sculpture in low cement relief, from sand moulds. The sides of the ramps, and the retaining walls, have running patterns like those on the borders of carpets, pleasant but repetitive. But the monolithic ramp-supports have distinct and individual semi-abstract, semi-representational figures on them, many of great beauty, others purely grotesque.

None of the ramps, none of the criss-crossing roadways, one on top of another, go anywhere, and their roadbeds are filled with great lumps of damp mud. The connecting roads haven't been built, so that this piece of architectural triumph is at the moment an exercise in design without function, of the most alarming kind. If you look at it long enough, it starts to scare you, and for miles on each side nothing justifies it, as though our civilization had either by-passed it and rejected it, or hadn't yet reached it. In two words, it's monstrous.

Staring out of his window, relaxing without thinking, Thierry felt the monstrous power and impersonality of life in this place and was oppressed by it. When he fell asleep, he dreamed of unglassed windows like eyes in mad heads; he saw the girl quit the bus, turn the corner or cross the street, or go off into fields – where had she gone? He strained after her all night, and awoke unrefreshed.

Naturally he hoped and expected – perhaps not fully aware of it – to see her again, and inevitably he did, under almost identical circumstances. Same kind of night, but a bit colder. Same time of night because he was working late very often, as the store worked into the early fall sales pattern. Same feelings of mixed languor, depression, and sleepy fatigue.

It was about two weeks later, after the first of the month because he'd just been paid; his commissions were spectacular and soon there would be no reason why he should not live on a more enlarged scale. When the bus drew near Pie-IX he let his head slump on his shoulder almost with expectancy, sure that she'd show herself again; this time he'd make sure that he saw where she went. He might even speak to her … speak … he began to hear rain … almost home.

A bell rang in his head. He sat up instantly and looked at the sidewise seat by the front door, and there she was with the light shining on her vinyl. Should he say something? As he stood up the bus lurched forward and gained speed, running down the street to the last stop. He steadied himself against an aluminum pole and opened his mouth, and as he did so she turned her head, lifting her pretty chin. Green flashed at her throat.

There was nobody else in the bus, and this time she saw him, no question about it, and she looked him full in the face and smiled an inviting smile, unmistakably meant for him. He glanced behind him to make sure there was nobody there; the bus stopped while his head was turned. In an instant she was out the door, her heels making their clack clack clack as she disappeared.

He pushed through the rear door impatiently and ran to the corner. She was nowhere in sight. Stupefied, and ignoring the laugh of the bus-driver, he ran diagonally across the intersection to the Saint-Léonard shopping centre, where he pressed his face against the glass door to the drugstore. The druggist, sensing an emergency, came across the deserted store and opened it.

'Where is she? Did she come in here?'

'Who?'

'A girl in a raincoat, green scarf, dark hair, all shining.'

'There's no girl here. What is this, anyway?' The druggist backed away, lifting his arms in alarm. Thierry loped down the sidewalk along the row of store windows, looked into the Chinese restaurant farther along, then into the recesses of two dark stores, still untenanted in the infant plaza. Nobody there. He crossed the parking lot and stood on the corner of rue Valdombre, a few feet behind the standing bus.

Across the street a sign read: BRIGHT FUTURE CONSTRUCTION.

He spotted the faint lights of the isolated duplexes on rue D'Avila, last outpost of civilization, and for some reason was certain she hadn't gone in there. Then he walked out to the end of Bélanger and followed the muddy and rutted lane out into the fields. A mile to the north, the lights of the Trans-Canada could be seen, and away off to the southeast there were stretches of almost invisible housing along Sherbrooke East. Directly in front of him there was nothing but dark fields and the lane which led down to a wide depression in the ground, something like a gravel pit or quarry several miles in width, and now that he was some distance east of the city, a deep pit of shadow. To his left lay the gutted body of a car, tilted on the edge of a twenty-foot drop in the ground. He picked his way towards it, treading carefully over stones and pieces of planking, and avoiding deep pools of muddy water; it was spitting rain and growing cooler.

He put his head in a glassless window of the ruined car, trying to see if there was anything inside. 'Are you in there?' he whispered. The interior of the car was suddenly dimly illuminated, which surprised him until he realized that the searchlight on top of the mountain was sending its revolving beam overhead; he waited till it came round again, lighting the car with pale reflection. Nobody there, coiled springs in the back seat, through the glove compartment you could see the ground. He backed away with a shiver of distaste for the car's corpse, turned and circled back, looking for the dirt track.

He must have descended a roll in the ground, because he couldn't see any lights, everything was darkness and cooling mist. He went on, uncertain of his bearings and careful of his footing on the sloping ground. In a moment he felt it straighten out and grow smooth, which meant that he was on the wide floor of the quarry, half a mile from the edge of town. It ought to be easy to walk back and forth till he came to the place where the road entered this space; then he would retrace his way until he saw some lights, simple, easy. The searchlight flashed overhead again in a consoling sort of way – there was no chance of losing his way. Where had she gone?

He looked up at the sky to catch the next revolution of the beam, to time it and notice its direction. The mist was a bit thicker. There it came: one second, two seconds, three ... he counted carefully and decided that it rotated once a minute, and was coming from where? Over there. No, over there. No. Wait a minute, catch it while it spins; too fast. One second, two ... here it comes.

He stared intently into the mist overhead, his head spinning and his eyes misted. Green. There she was. As the beam of light traversed the mist he saw gathered over him in the sky a cloud, a bank of fog, what? Her image taking shape as the light passed overhead. He saw her plain as day, green scarf, impalpable filmy coat. Then he bent his head and walked as fast as he could towards the searchlight, not looking up again. The ground rose under him, a hillside at last. He struggled upwards, gasping, and was standing in somebody's backyard, rue D'Avila. Some doors away a dog began to bark, which made him feel irrationally guilty, like some sort of prowler. He trotted down a driveway and onto the newly paved roadway, from where he could see the shopping centre and bus stop which he loved and needed.

He didn't want any more adventures like that – too unusual and revelatory, so he changed the time he left the store, quitting sharp at nine and hurrying home with plenty of people around him to keep him awake and less subject to hallucination. He never saw her in the 95 bus again; it was all a mistake; he just needed a little rest, some recreation, something to vary his routine. Now and then he borrowed his uncle's car and went for a ride in the suburbs, looking at houses or exploring new roads; the way the city grew and spread fascinated him. It sprouted like something alive. This month there were dozens of families living on crescents where last month there had been nothing. When he drove on the Trans-Canada, he took care at first to go no further than the inhabited east end, and he wasn't a superstitious or fearful man.

And then one night, well into the fall, he made his crucial gesture, driving onto the Trans-Canada at Pie-IX and putting his head an inch too close to the noose. He drove east from the interchange with a certain pride, some vague idea in his mind of defeating an irrational phobia. And then he saw her shooting past him at fantastic speed, alone on a motorcycle, scarf streaming like a banner, unmistakably his girl; he'd have known her anywhere, and he took up the chase with a shout of recognition, putting his foot down to the floor.

His car had plenty of acceleration, but she must have had one damn fine motorcycle; she flew ahead of him incredibly fast, out of town, beyond the built-up areas, and then the taillight of the motorcycle flickered and disappeared and he realized where she was going. He was alone on the highway and gave his car all it would take. In five minutes he saw the lunatic circuits and whirls of the Montée de Saint-Léonard interchange spinning up in front of him like magical spiderweb. He hit the brakes and pulled the car up to the stop sign like a television cop, and there, right over there against one of the monstrous uprights, under a ramp leading nowhere, he saw the motorcycle, or at least some motorcycle, parked beside a dizzy semi-abstract sculpture of a woman. He ran his car deep into the mud under the interchange, leaped out and ran to the motorcycle. The engine was still hot. She must be here somewhere. He glanced around distractedly and saw a ramp entry, fifty feet off into twilight; he ran over and tried to see footprints, too dark. Then he walked up the ramp; a higher ramp crossed overhead, then he was under another, and circling arcs of concrete were all around him like tentacles. He came high up onto what he thought was the main overpass and tried to see along its whole length. Which way to go? He forgot at once which way he'd turned, and came immediately to a frail unlighted barrier and a precipitous drop. He looked down and the pattern of interlaced curves was too much for him, vertiginous. He sat in the mud, then crawled away from the edge on his hands and knees. When he stood up again, he saw that he was on a part of the overpass where the guardrails hadn't been installed, so he went to his knees once more. Too dark. Heavy mud.

He crawled abreast of a ramp, wondered passively if this was the one he'd climbed, and if his car would still be there when he came down. Down this ramp slowly, car nowhere to be seen. Up another ramp, crawl, don't walk, might fall. In half an hour he was completely exhausted. He wanted to sleep, but lifted his head a last time to stare at a figure on a massive concrete slab rising before him. On it was some ghastly design. He thought, it looks like a test-pattern. But what it really was, if he could have seen it in the right light, was a peculiarly distorted concrete woman.

Starting Again on Sherbrooke Street

'YUDEL, YUDEL, why'd you sell your bus? We need it now.'

'The bottom fell out, you know that. It seemed unsafe.'

'This is not going to work. I have eighteen canvases to go in that little bug, plus drawings, no. I can't risk it. I'll have to hire a truck, another expense. That's all right, don't feel bad. I forgive you, the expense is nothing … a poor painter.'

'You mean an unfortunate painter.'

Seymour started to chuckle. 'Poor and unfortunate both. Do you really think they'll fit?'

'Sure they will. Look, the back seat folds down, all kinds of room, three and a half by four and a half. You shouldn't paint any bigger than that anyway.'

'I may become a muralist.'

'Not in my car.' I folded down the seat and hooked it in place, at the same time opening the door as wide as possible, making a cavernous gap. 'A cavernous gap,' I said, and we both laughed helplessly. 'You bring them down, and I'll put them in.'

'Two flights of stairs.'

'All right then, I'll bring them down and you put them in; we can't leave them standing here alone.'

'It's true,' said Seymour, 'a genuine Segal is irreplaceable.'

'Maybe not valuable, but irreplaceable.'

'Both.'

I said, 'Go bring them down; then I'll take a turn, that's fair.' I heard him run upstairs and in a minute he stuck his head out of the studio window and called down, 'Could I maybe throw them to you?'

'Stop clowning, we've got work to do. And bring the big ones first.' He went away from the window and I said out loud, 'Why does he have to paint so big?' A passer-by stopped and looked at me curiously and then went into the restaurant next door. I saw him talking to the counterman and eyeing me. Then Seymour brought out the first of the paintings, none of them sober imitations of the natural scene, and the man in the restaurant looked at it, then at me, caught my eye. There is something deeply compromising about trying to load an outsized work of art into a Volkswagen. I felt the man's eyes on my neck as I worked the canvas into the baggage space, a tight fit.

'I use thin canvas,' said Seymour, 'I think they'll go.' But it took us an hour to place them carefully, making sure that they weren't going to slide and rub against each other. The drawings sat neatly on top.

'Now drive like the wind,' said Seymour.

'I will, hell,' I said, 'if they start to shift they'll be in here on our necks, and the rear window is blocked and I'm using the side mirrors. Which way should we go?' We were at the studio on Lagauchetière just west of Bleury, out of the high-rent district, and were delivering the paintings to Abe Shumsky's gallery on Sherbrooke for Seymour's fall show, his most important show so far.

'Galerie Anéantie,' said Seymour.

'I know all about that.'

'On Sherbrooke, almost directly across from the museum.'

'Is there an alley behind?'

'Oh, come on, I'll pay all fines.'

'Correct!' I drove down to Craig and along towards Guy, keeping out of the mid-town traffic and staying mostly in second gear. We came north on Guy past the luxury motels corner Dorchester and up to Sherbrooke, turned with the green and drove east.

Abreast of the museum Seymour said, 'There's a space.'

'I can't park here, don't be silly.'

'Sure you can; it's a commercial shipment.' He leaped out the door.

'First I'd heard of it.' I saw the lettering in the windows, up a short flight of stairs from the sidewalk. GALERIE ANÉANTIE. There was a somewhat dramatized photograph of Seymour in a corner of one window. I got out and went around the car, keeping an eye open for the traffic detail, leaving the emergency lights blinking – might as well act commercial, I thought. I put the drawings in the front seat, extracted the top painting and stood it beside me so as to look like a deliveryman.

Sherbrooke Street looked wonderful in the October sunlight. It always does at that time of year, when you can feel the cycle of the year starting up again, the big fall shows in the galleries, girls in highly novel clothes, the hockey season starting in the Forum a few blocks west. Boutiques full of whatever it is they sell, and antique shops likewise – Sherbrooke is where you find them. It was an afternoon full of the future.

Forty years ago, or even twenty, Sherbrooke Street was impressive in quite a different way, a classically dignified enclave of great houses and tall old shade trees, gravelled carriage drives and wrought-iron gates, the southern boundary of the famous 'square mile' of wealth. The 'good' part of the street stretched farther in those days, and now that things are so much changed the parts west of Guy and east of Metcalfe though still sprinkled with handsome buildings aren't part of the essential Sherbrooke.

The real thing starts at Peel and runs past Stanley, Drummond, Mountain, Crescent, Bishop, Mackay, to Guy, seven blocks in all. The north side is almost entirely given over to those great houses which have become the headquarters of important social institutions like Corby Distilleries, to tall office buildings and apartment blocks, to a fashionable church, and to the Montréal Museum of Fine Arts.

On the south side there are twelve private galleries. As Seymour said reflectively during his first museum show, 'They come out of there, they go across the street and see something of yours for sale in a gallery, who knows?' Around the museum and its flock of baby chicks, the galleries, are clustered the antique shops and boutiques, like the widening waves produced by dropping a stone in calm water. And then there is the Ritz, just where it ought to be in the middle of all this, in the block between Drummond and Mountain. I admire the neat striations produced by the proximity of money: pictures, antiques, lovely women, a hotel called the Ritz (what else), no taverns and no automobile showrooms. I often wonder who sets the tone and rules out the undesirable elements.

Seymour came down to the sidewalk with Mr. Shumsky, whom I knew slightly, and we shook hands, and then all three of us began to trot into the gallery with pictures in our arms. I thought, it's a good thing nobody's burglarizing the museum this afternoon. I could imagine an assistant curator dashing down the steps. 'Stop thief, help, murder, police!' Me and Seymour flat on our faces while Mr. Shumsky tried to explain us away to a French policeman. Thought influences action. While I was resting beside the car, heaving a deep breath, a patrol car came along and a cop stuck his head out the window, considering whether or not to give us a ticket. I grinned feebly and he got out, came to the curb and examined the picture I was balancing on the sidewalk, an enormous, blue, three-headed, nightmarish, screaming figure. His expression changed.

'Vous faites de la peinture, vous?'

'Ah non, c'est un copain, un grand talent, je crois. Par-là.' I pointed to the windows of the gallery where Seymour and Mr. Shumsky were now arguing about positioning the pictures. I wished they would join me.

'Ah hé, je le connais bien, c'est le petit homme de Lagauchetière, correct?' It turned out that he used to patrol the warehouse district on the night shift.

'C'est ça, c'est ça.' Seymour now came out and whacked the cop on the shoulder, and another person joined the group, a tall, conservatively dressed gent with an expensive dark suit, a rolled umbrella, a fancy grey vest with piping at the edges and a distinctly military moustache.

'At it again, eh?' said this man, referring to my wild and criminal past.

'Christopher, don't you ever do any work?'

'Got-to-meet-a-client-for-a-drink.' I knew him fairly well; he had something to do with a brokerage house, I think, or possibly one of the really grand retail establishments dealing in English clothes or silver. Christopher Holt. He stood faintly smiling as Seymour finished his talk with the policeman, feinted a left hook at him and saw him into the patrol car, which then drove off.

'Seymour, this is Christopher Holt. You might have met already.'

'Once, with you, at the hockey game,' said Seymour.

Christopher pointed his umbrella at the blue screamer appraisingly. 'This is what you're doing now, is it? I saw your first show across the street.' He had an absurd air of connoisseurship, unsupported by information. Seymour was looking at me across Christopher's line of vision and I could tell from the lift of his eyebrows what he was thinking. *This is the guy?* The subject of a sadly funny history. He certainly was the guy.

I met Christopher at the Forum, where I used to stand behind him at the top of the Terrace seats, the cheapest standing room available, buck and a quarter on sale the night of the game. I saw about thirty home games plus playoffs every season at a very modest cost, always standing in the same spot, immediately behind Christopher and his guest of the evening, whoever that might be, usually a female. After I'd shouted down their necks, alternately in English and ludicrous French, for a few seasons, he and his guests began to talk to me, first to ask if I could be quieter or shout upwards, then to discuss the game, finally to talk about mutual acquaintances.

Half the time he brought to the game a young woman whom I early identified as his wife, neat, quiet, very intelligent, attractive, and interesting rather than pretty, a very senior medical researcher at Montréal General. Once or twice a season he would bring his uncle. The rest of the time he had another girl along, probably a cousin, I thought, because the design of the bones of her face, the cheeks and jaw, strongly resembled him, and there was something intimate and of long standing about their association. Once when he had his wife with him, a bit confused in my mind, I said, 'I haven't seen your cousin for a while,' without specifying the sex of this person.

'What cousin is that, Chris?' asked his wife pleasantly.

'You must mean my *uncle* .'

'Ah,' I said, 'I was a bit mixed up. Of course, he does look quite a bit older than you.' Between periods he got me alone with him, going for hotdogs or something, and gave me military-type blast. He was a reserve major in a distinguished regiment. 'Idiot. Dolt. Conehead. Big mouth. Where are your brains?'

'Not your cousin, eh?'

'I may be promiscuous, but I am not incestuous.'

She was his – what – popsy, girl friend? 'Mistress' always sounds such a pompous thing to be, as a celebrated author has pointed out. Anyway she was that, had been for two years, and their relation was now at its fullest development, perhaps about to wane. Christopher wanted, and did not want, to forsake the familiar comforts of the luxurious apartment just up the mountain off Côte des Neiges which he and his wife shared – they had no children. This apartment was in a very imposing district, with a tame English peer living across the street from the Holts – to give the place a kind of tone, I suppose.

He wanted to go with Elena but could not bring himself to take the leap and had been vacillating at that point for a year, to the extreme annoyance of Elena on the one hand, and his wife (whom he supposed ignorant of the affair) on the other.

After they found out – I didn't tell them – that I was a writer, Christopher and his wife used to ask me some of those questions that people do.

'Where do your stories come out?'

They were not familiar with the magazines where my stories came out.

'Where do you get your ideas from anyway?'

There's an answer to that question but it never satisfies anybody. However, I gave it to them in all its banality.

'All around me; there's a story in everybody around us.' We were at the hockey game when I said this, and Christopher looked around him at the sellout crowd.

'Fifteen thousand stories?'

'Work for a lifetime,' I said smugly. 'You should see my notebook. I'll never write them all.'

They seemed disbelieving, and after that did not ask many questions about those of my activities which did not touch them. We became friendly; sometimes I went to their place after the games for tea, and once Christopher showed me his bearskin in its towering hatbox.

'It takes a whole bear,' he said enthusiastically.

'Like ordering elephant steak in a gourmet restaurant?'

'Something like that,' he said with a grin. Then while Ruth was out of the room, he told me something about his personal affairs.

'Elena won't wait much longer,' he said, 'and now she's seeing a guy with tickets downstairs in the mezzanine. I always knew I should have changed.'

I was noncommittal, thinking of my notebook.

'What do you think I should do?'

The big temptation in my line of work is to observe without emotional commitment, which in time atrophies your feelings, whereupon your observations lose their juice, dry up, then you're left with nothing but anthropology. I felt I ought to say something, even the wrong thing, and yet I knew I couldn't win. In any case, I didn't really know him well, a few beers together in the Forum Tavern, tea at their apartment, and about a thousand hockey games. Not sufficient evidence to form a judgement. I said, 'I don't think I should say anything, Christopher,' and felt like a fink. I had no idea what he should do, but maybe I ought to have taken a blind shot, and the consequent responsibility, for the sake of magnanimity.

'I don't know you well enough, and I hardly know Ruth at all.' Fortunately his wife came back into the room at that moment, and I was spared further cross-examination.

The drift of his feelings was plain; he wanted Elena, whom he considered more sexually adequate than his wife, and he hoped that somebody would push him off the dock. I didn't want to be the one who did it, and I guess other people felt the same way. The moment for decision passed; spring brought the playoffs, and I didn't see him again till early fall, when he started calling me up to see if I wanted his second hockey ticket; apparently his wife had always been bored stiff by the game, and he no longer felt like obliging her to accompany him. Sometimes I bought the tickets, sometimes he didn't call, and I knew that he would be bringing Elena with him; then she was less in evidence. And then one night he missed most of the first period – of a Toronto game at that – and when he finally appeared he was unsober and in an emotional turmoil.

'Pulford got a quick goal,' I said.

'Elena has left me,' he said, 'and she's going to marry that guy with the good seats.'

'Not just because of that?'

He lurched into his seat and patted the one next to him. 'Sit down, sit down, nobody's coming; you might as well have it as anybody.'

I had already paid for standing room and was not eager to

pay for a ticket as well – see how little other people's tragedies affect us? 'Let me pay you for it,' I said hypocritically.

'Naw, naw. I should have left her. If only I'd left her when I should have.' He looked at me accusingly, making me conscious of strong guilt-feelings. Can you have guilt-feelings without guilt?

I said, 'You remember asking where I got my stories?'

'Yeah, I see, this is how. Must make you feel a bit parasitical.'

I was unprepared for this flash of perception and was left with my mouth hanging open, just as Ron Ellis scored the Leafs' second goal.

'Looks like a bad night,' said Christopher, 'I'll leave her tomorrow.'

And he did. Over the pleas of his mother and family and all Ruth's friends; he got out of his comfortable home just at the wrong time, a few months too late, and took a hideous one-room bachelor apartment in one of the new 'luxury' buildings on Sherbrooke west of Guy. These places are supposed to be the successors of the great houses of Sherbrooke, co-operative apartments in huge buildings in a geographical area where rich people have always lived. Judging by Christopher's apartment, which was in one of the most expensive buildings, this is a retrograde step in urban life-style. What it resembled more than anything else to my eyes was a cell.

The kitchen scarcely existed at all, I suppose because bachelors are notorious diners-out. The living room was a stark rectangle about twelve by eighteen, the walls painted in a muddy taupe, with a concrete slab projecting from the foot of the only window, a flimsy rail around it, the balcony which is mandatory to Montréal apartments. The whole problem in such a place is to avoid doing anything more than sleeping in it, and to form an ironclad habit of making up the bed first thing in the morning. Otherwise madness beckons.

He gave a wine-and-cheese plus gin-and-tonic party there, to which I was invited, the only time I was in the place. The guests were officers from his regiment and their girls, some people living in the building, a department-store executive and his wife, altogether around twenty people in this little pen. We had to leave the hall and balcony doors open to avoid asphyxiation, and at that it was stuffy. When the other guests began to go, Christopher asked me to stick around for a bit.

'What do you think of my place?'

'I hate it,' I said, frank for perhaps the first time in our acquaintance.

'It costs a lot.'

'I don't want to know what it costs.'

'But they say you can get your equity out pretty quickly.'

I thought, 'Oh, oh.'

'In addition to the purchase price, there's the maintenance fee,' he said, 'You're right. It isn't a good deal.' It was the only time he ever praised my financial acumen, and that was just, because I have none. I could see the trend of his reasoning. Elena had *not* married the man with the blue tickets, but she had also refused to see anything more of Christopher, who had simply kept her on the hook too long. He claimed she even used the phrase 'best years of my life.'

He sat on his unaired day bed and said, 'She needs me. It's cruel, you know.'

'Who needs you?'

'Ruth. She has no life of her own apart from the lab. It seems a shame to think of her all alone up there. I give her a hundred and a quarter a month to help out, which isn't easy, because in my bracket I have to earn twice that to give it to her.'

'You're lucky,' I said, 'it's a privilege to pay high taxes.'

He scowled unpleasantly; we had nothing in common politically. 'I'm considering going back to her, only I'm afraid it would just lead to more of the same in a year, and besides I'm doing all right, I'm getting girls and having fun.' He was in the most perfect state of indecision I'd ever seen, like Buridan's ass between two bundles of hay of equal magnitude, a paralysing and unmanning situation.

Sometimes he thought that Elena would take up with him again, and looking at their relation from outside I thought he might be right, until I remembered how, in my adolescence, girl after girl had stopped going out with me after a while. None of them ever revoked her decision. It seems that once sexual attraction has been dissipated in the female, it seldom or never revives. Why is that? What ever goes through a woman's head in those circumstances – sensations of physical distaste, moral revulsion – was going through Elena's. Even poetry was no help.

'I suddenly found myself writing the stuff,' Christopher would say, 'and you know it scanned and everything. I sent it to her office, and it may do some good.' But it didn't; the banked fires of love wouldn't unbank.

'Jesus, I'm desperate,' he would say, between periods at the hockey games, which is where Seymour heard his story, commenting to me afterwards that it was classical in proportion.

'Falling between two stools,' said Seymour.

'You could put it more elegantly,' I said, 'but you've got it by the right handle.'

This is the guy, isn't it? We looked at each other while Christopher analysed the painting I held in front of me, placing it in the context of Seymour's *oeuvre*, tracing the main lines of the composition with the point of his neat umbrella and saying how much he admired the colours. He certainly did his best to be complimentary, and under the rays of his approval Seymour unbent a bit.

'Come to the show when we've got it hung, and tell me how you like it.' An extraordinary concession.

'I will indeed.'

'Where are you living now, Christopher?' I asked.

'Back at the old place on the hill.'

'With your wife?'

'Certainly. Taking a fresh grip on things, you know, fresh start. The right time of year for it.' He sniffed the fine afternoon air appreciatively, shouldered his umbrella, said a few more nice things to Seymour and turned to go. 'Ruth will be with me at the games this year,' he said, 'can you manage?'

'I think so.'

'Good. Be seeing you then.'

We stood on the sidewalk and watched him stroll in the direction of the Ritz, tall, well-dressed, confident, untouched, a Sherbrooke Street man.

Predictions of Ice

GREAT CITIES ARE BUILT on the shore or by important crossroads or on a hill. 'Montréal,' says the geography book, 'is built on four islands formed by the confluence of the Ottawa and the Saint Lawrence. The chief topographical prominence of the largest island is the hill or mountain for which the city is named. Volcanic as late as the Palaeolithic, its crater may still be seen, the "Beaver Lake" of a popular mountaintop park.' Here are the shore and the hill of the great city, and I suppose that for 'crossroads' we can substitute 'railway junction' and 'airport'.

Of the alternatives, a shore location has always been allowed first place; if a city has no port it must fall back on secondary claims to consequence. Think of all the cities at the mouths of rivers or in their estuaries. If there is one thing we've got in Montréal, it's shoreline, the mouth of the Ottawa and the beginning of the estuary of the Saint Lawrence.

The great river doesn't widen radically here, but it is so broad and deep that it is fully navigable at the port by all but the newest and largest ships. The last year or two, along with every other port on the Seaway, we've been troubled by low water. Sometimes the water chart has required temporary revision, but the ships have continued to come and the city still derives its importance largely from the harbour.

I'm speaking of logical priorities, not strictly of dollars expended. It could be argued that the financial activity in the city, or the heavy industry, or the railways and airlines, or even the goings-on in the arts, must take precedence over ship transport, but the city wouldn't be here in the first place if it weren't for the port. It's still cheaper and safer and easier to ship or travel by water than any other way, especially where bulk shipment is involved. Try to send fifty million bushels of wheat to Russia in late November by air! Like drinking a bucket of beer with an eye-dropper. Try to move three divisions of troops plus supporting formations by rail or air to some obscure country you wish to liberate! Your war of liberation will be tedious indeed.

Where the Ottawa and the Saint Lawrence meet, at Lac des Deux Montagnes and Lac Saint-Louis, they gradually invest and surround four islands, Ile Perrot in the west, to the north small Ile Bizard and big Ile Jésus, in the centre and east the island of Montréal itself, a northern Venice. There are rivers and canals and bridges – my God, the dozens of bridges – all over the place. Though you may live in the centre of town and go to work for twenty years up and down the same bus line, without a glimpse of water, you can't help sensing it all around you. It's no accident that the big river has a saint's name; there's something godlike about the rivers....

The Saint Lawrence is mysteriously invisible for miles along the shore, unless you have a special vantage point. You can be a hundred yards away and unable to see it, and the reason of course is the extraordinary density of the port installations. There are four major bridges connecting Montréal island with the south shore: the Mercier, Champlain, Victoria, Jacques-Cartier; and a fifth, a combination bridge and tunnel, is being built some distance farther east. Besides these huge commercial and industrial links, all around the island there are smaller ones, four lanes, two lanes, leading to the suburbs and the country. But the five principal bridges frame the port and the money; between the Mercier and the new Boucherville complex lie several hundred millions of dollars, worth of grain elevators, meat packing and shipping plants, railway sidings, drydocks, ship-yards, warehousing, fantastic mobile cranes, customs services, wharfage, some of it of remarkable delicacy and complexity, cold storage plants, automobile massing and storage yards. Make you think of London or New York? That's my object.

Let's start with Bridge Street, a good name and a good location, sometimes almost impossible to reach. If I were standing on the corner of McGill and Wellington near the menacing silhouette of the Customs House, thinking perhaps of trying to claim a parcel they're holding on me, and an ill-advised stranger asked me how to get to Bridge Street, I'd have to make the classic reply, 'I wouldn't start from here.'

There's a lot of new highway and access-road construction going forward there; from one day to the next, you don't know where the barricades and the holes in the roads, and the detours, and the traffic policeman, half out of their minds, are going to be. But supposing that we find ourselves on Bridge Street a few hundred feet south of the Mill Street intersection (*quelle hardiesse*), we'll be about at the beginning of the thickest and richest deposit of port and rail facilities imaginable. What you see from here are the immense grain elevators and some of the meat handling warehouses: rivers, bread, meat, nothing more human. The proof lies in the magnificence, the grand scale, of these buildings, among the noblest works of man, the means by which a people is fed.

Coming east along Mill Street towards Commissioner and Place Royale, we begin to discern a different aspect of the port, the unloading arrangements for industrial and package freight. Farther east again, down a bumpy incline and under a tunnel, can be found the cheerful little dock where for fifty years excursion steamers put out for the celebrated Saguenay cruises, now unhappily a thing of the past. They used to leave to the sound of a brass band, with a happy crowd at dockside to bid all voyagers Godspeed, as if they were crossing the Atlantic instead of carting their golf clubs down to Murray Bay. Once at the end of a sweltering summer I stood at the extreme edge of that wharf and watched the wedding-cake shape of one of those steamers, the *Tadoussac* or the *Richelieu*, float off illuminated into a soft grey twilight, all lights blazing, band playing, faint shouts of good cheer ringing across calm water. The river opened before her, under the great Jacques-Cartier she went, broad-beamed and dignified, softly outlined, gone.

Here are the Cunard docks, and how they ever get twenty-five thousand tons of liner in there is beyond me. You wouldn't want to take a thirty-foot power cruiser into that maze of slips unless you'd had a few runs at it in broad daylight, with some tugboat skipper hollering derisive instructions at you from a dockside vantage point.

Away east under the Jacques-Cartier to more advantageously located and more crowded docking space along about Berth 39. This is where naval craft tie up on ceremonial visits to the city. Lately we've had French, American, and most recently Brazilian squadrons in the harbour – leave for the sailors and a civic reception for the officers. I once escorted my kids over a

French destroyer in port for a four-day official call, and open for public inspection. My daughter Sarah spied an open porthole on the maindeck and asked to look through it. She and I stuck our heads through – it was quite a large opening – and there in the wardroom a French officer was sneaking a solitary Scotch before coping with the herds of visitors. Our heads suddenly appeared just as he raised his glass, and he spilled half the drink down the front of an otherwise immaculate uniform jacket. I grinned apologetically and Sarah laughed a lot.

'We sure surprised him, didn't we, Dad?'

'Yeah, honey.'

Berth 39 and its neighbours are right out on the river, not in artificially constructed ship canals or slips, so they are easy to get at. A lot of automobiles are unloaded here, Opels, Peugeots, Skodas, Datsuns, and parked in blocks of several hundred to be trucked away. When the longshoremen were on strike in the crucial summer of 1966, there were cars everywhere you looked, which couldn't be moved.

Les débardeurs sont en grève! That summer the life of the city came close to being throttled, as hundreds of ships, clear down to Québec, waited in line for the strike to be settled so they could be unloaded. A dock strike is a classic dramatic situation, written about and filmed numberless times, and the longshoremen's unions are frequent targets for bitter attack; sometimes there is violence. *Les débardeurs sont en grève!* They're one of the keys to our lives, as farmers are, and most of the time we don't remember. That's likely why trouble on the docks is endemic to the modern city. Considering their importance, the longshoremen are underpaid, overworked and harassed from within their unions as well as from outside by conflicting claims and divided loyalties.

Trouble on the docks can start from the most insignificant causes; the strike in the summer of sixty-six started when the police began to ticket longshoremen's cars. Immemorial custom dictates that they park on the docks, close to their work, ready to move a mile or so to the next job. But harbour law limits parking stringently – right there you've got an explosive situation. When the police started handing out tickets, it made a perfect pretext for grievance, strike, violence.

I can bear witness to the violence from direct observation. I love the docks and the ships and have spent hours and hours poking around, learning what the installations are used for, this crane, that mobile elevator, where the ships come from, what they carry. A friend of mine, Don McMahon, works for the principal Canadian flour processer, a company whose name is a household word. They mill various grains but mainly wheat, shipping it in the form of flour, in bags, in bulk, in endless qualities and grades. Don knows all about the violence on the docks. Grain in bulk and its products, particularly high-grade flour, are keys to life. It's as simple as that. Where some basic commodity is traded in, we find want, desperation, faction, greed, and violence, for the usual human reasons. Men need bread; other men wish to profit from this. The wheat goes off the docks into holds through potential explosion.

When the Canadian Wheat Board concluded the famous Russian wheat sale – two hundred and twenty-two million bushels worth four hundred and fifty million dollars – a couple of years back, the story was reported in the papers as an unqualified boon to the Canadian farmer, the processer, the shipper, the maritime industries. But when you look at the sale a bit more closely than the newspaper stories allowed, you see at once the incredible problems involved. The grain had to be harvested, shipped by rail to the Lakehead, trans-shipped into bulk carriers for carriage through the Seaway to Montréal, processed, some of it, into flour, trans-shipped again to the ocean-going vessels bound for the Russian port of entry. When such a complex system is in play right down to the end of the shipping season, those last crucial days before the freeze, at the end of November, when those final fifty million bushels have to be loaded before the ice comes, and when there are active and powerful interests with grievances because of some feature of the deal – what happens?

One dark, cold, wet night at the end of November, I was cruising around the docks in my car, playing my favourite, rather immature, game of imagining myself a character in some spy or detective movie. Down on Mill Street after nine o'clock, the size of the elevators and the absence of human figures, the way the shadows fall and envelop you, the way your footsteps echo in the narrow street, all require your imagination to cast you as a man on the run, skulking in doorways, a hunted fugitive about to sneak aboard ship with the plans, or else to exchange shots with agents on the other side.

I drove slowly along Mill to the bridge over the old canal and turned right, towards the dockside. A sign there says ENTRÉE INTERDITE but nobody ever pays any attention to such signs on the docks, and I've spent many happy hours there under the elevators, wishing I had a camera and a contract for a film. Between the elevators and the edge of the docks runs some peculiar trackage, recessed into the ground and with a very wide gauge, much wider than railway track, maybe twelve feet across. Along these tracks moves the most grandiose of the port installations, so big that it reminds you of the scaffolding around a moon rocket, moved somewhat similarly except that rocketry installations move on huge tractor-treads instead of tracks. This thing, as tall as a twenty-storey building, can be shifted freely along its tracks to either end of the dock for loading purposes. I guess you'd call it a mobile elevator.

I parked beside it, got out of the car and turned my overcoat collar up, against the freezing rain. I sneaked over next to the great wheels of this gigantic device, moving in and out of shadow and admiring the way the scene made cinematic patterns of line and darkness. A hundred yards away at the other end of the slip the lights of an ocean-going vessel, moored for loading, shone in the darkness.

Suddenly I heard a harsh cry from that direction, followed by a strange shuffling noise and then the sound of running feet. I saw two dark figures cross the railway sidings and disappear towards Mill Street. I remembered that the last car I'd passed had been a patrol car, and hoped that it was somewhere around. I stood in the shadows filled with indecision, feeling foolishly as though I'd been unfairly projected out of my imaginings into a real-life movie. Then I walked quickly along the dock, well away from the water, making sure that nobody followed me. At first there wasn't a sound, and then as I came towards the faint lights of the ship I began to hear heavy and irregular breathing.

This was crazy. All my romantic ideas about the port were

now to be endorsed by actuality. I saw a man lying, or half kneeling, at the foot of the gangway leading to the ship's main-deck. The gangway was closed off by a heavy chain and a sign that was concealed by the man's body. I saw the name of the ship and her port of registry astern, but they were in Cyrillic lettering which made no sense to me.

I ran the last few feet to the man and knelt beside him, aware that I was sticking my nose into something potentially danger-ous, and the damnedest confusion of life imagined and life lived. The man had been beaten severely and was unconscious. Only the gangway chain kept him from complete collapse. He was a big heavy man and hard to move, but I took off my over-coat and folded it into a kind of pillow and laid it on the ground. Then I half lifted and half dragged the guy off the chain, and it was hard, just so much dead weight. With great difficulty I got him stretched out on his back, his head and shoulders resting on the coat. I noticed several pop bottles lying around on the dock and wondered if he'd been beaten with them, but when I looked at his head I saw that a bottle would have been smashed by such a hard blow. He'd been hit at least four or five times on the back and side of the head, and proba-bly twice on the face. There was a deep gash over his left eye-brow; the side of his face was swelling and the bruises were forming. He wore vaguely marine clothes, dark blue jacket and heavy sweater, thick trousers, some sort of rubberized boots. The light from the nearby lamp-post made his face look pretty awful. His breathing was irregular, and I began to be afraid he might die, and then what? He was certainly getting soaked, lying on his back in the rain.

I went to the gangway and shouted as loud as I could, 'Hello, *hello*, anybody on board, anybody there?'

Half a dozen men appeared instantly from different direc-tions on deck, which puzzled me. I'd heard this fellow cry out a hundred yards away. How come they weren't out here before me? Anyway they crowded down the gangway and spotted the man on the dock. One of them at once went back on board and returned with blankets and some brandy. Somebody else brought damp cloths to sponge off his face. They got some brandy into him, and the blankets around him, and one of them handed me my coat. They were doing a lot of talking in Russian, none in English, and none to me. They supported the injured man between them and took him on board, and that was the last I saw or heard of him.

The last sailor to go was dressed in an officer's jacket and something that looked like pyjama pants. I kept trying to ask him a lot of questions. 'Do you need me? To talk to the police? Do you want my name and address, should I do something about this, report it? What?'

He just gave me a polite brush.

I suppose I should have said something about it to the police, but I didn't. All next day I looked for some notice of the incident in the papers but there wasn't a word about it, not a line, nothing. One of the most puzzling things that's ever happened to me. In the afternoon I went around to Don McMahon's office to ask him what the hell, but before I said anything I asked him a few questions.

'How's the shipment going this year?'

'The Russian stuff?'

'Uh-huh.'

'We're in a bad spot. It looks like the freeze-up will be early this year, might even start with the cold front that's coming into town overnight. We've been driving and hurrying for weeks and now we're right up against the deadline, the first ice.'

'But the port will be open again in January?' There's hardly any off season in Montréal now, and another few years will see the end of the winter closing. Last year a specially reinforced Russian freighter made port the day after New Year's.

'We can't make significant shipments in vessels that size,' said Don, 'we've got to get it all out before the ice comes.'

'And you've been having trouble?'

'Trouble? We've had out-and-out sabotage.'

I gazed at him innocently. 'From what, where, who? Who wants to make trouble?'

'There's been a lot of opposition to this deal,' he said evasively, 'political opposition, union opposition, commercial discontent. We've had bulk shipments sabotaged by dead cats and mice, and broken glass.'

'Broken glass?'

'Yeah, broken bottles. Been a lot of complaints from the other side.'

I decided to keep my mouth shut.

'You'd think that shipping grain and flour to people would be as popular as could be, in this country,' Don said, 'but we've had hundreds, literally hundreds, of flour sacks slashed open during loading. How do you figure that?'

'Feeding the hungry,' I said, 'I seem to remember reading something about that somewhere.'

'Better look it up,' said Don, 'if it freezes up now, the deal is ruined.'

The next morning, the second day after the slugging incident, I drove well out east to where I had an unimpeded view of the river and the main ship channel. There had been very low temperatures overnight, and it was the first of December. Sure enough the river was covered with the first thin sheet of ice. Unless the cold spell broke tonight, ship traffic would be over in less than a week. I stood on the dock and watched a freighter moving slowly eastward, careful of even this much ice. Her silhouette was familiar; so was her ensign. I think she may have had an acquaintance of mine on board.

It was extremely cold and the ice seemed to thicken visibly as I stared at it. I watched the Russian freighter out of sight, then turned to go. This cold would not break over night; the year was over.

The River Behind Things

RIVIÈRE-DES-PRAIRIES on the north side of the island, unlike the Saint Lawrence, is accessible; you can see it, live with it, even float on it for most of its length, from Senneville to Pointe-aux-Trembles, although there's a power dam at Laval-des-Rapides which cuts it in half. To the east of the dam there's a lot of pollution – the watercourse serves two million people. But the head of this little stream at the extreme west of the island, rising out of Lac des Deux Montagnes, remains pure. Here you might even drink it. Certainly you can swim or run a small power boat, maintain a summer cottage or a beach resort.

The north shore is rimmed by Highway 37 which has a certain expansiveness, even grandeur, in its urban stretches; in the countryside it dwindles to a narrow two-lane highway, curving capriciously and reminiscent, in its defective engineering, of the nineteen-twenties. To the east, past Montréal-Nord, the road runs through full country, fields, farmhouses, and the river alongside, with here and there a landing where you can fish, though you won't catch much on account of pollution. There are in fact a few fish left alive in the turbid water.

Once on a summer Sunday we took the children out east to fish with bent pin and string at the waterside; they couldn't get their lines into deep water. There are reeds and extensive garbage deposits along the shore. But a man a few feet away from us, who was doing a little rudimentary casting, actually managed to land a somnolent and outsized catfish, several pounds in weight. The children were astonished and delighted; the catch mitigated the afternoon heat. There must have been hundreds of people fishing there that day, none hoping for a full creel but all enjoying themselves. You wouldn't take an aqualung below the surface at this point but at least the river *is* reachable, and there are other, uncontaminated, parts of it.

The northwest of the island has retained its pastoral character because until recently there was no bridge up there. All that is changed now. The Trans-Canada Highway has been joined to the mainland at Sainte-Anne-de-Bellevue by a grand new span linking important new highway connections with Ottawa and Toronto. With this development the pastoral scene must inevitably be transformed. Already ribbon development, light industrial plants, distributing warehouses, shopping centres, real-estate development are creeping west and north along the service roads feeding the main highway. Some years from now the open land will be gone; this is inevitable and not to be deplored. What replaces the farms will in time acquire its own charm. I'm not much persuaded by the saw 'Where every prospect pleases, and only man is vile'. The pleasure of the prospect depends upon the viewer and his sense of the appropriateness of the setting to certain forms of human action. Landscape has no special grace in itself.

But the changes take some getting used to. The well-known breeder, trainer, and owner, Jimmy Langill, has a farm up there in the northwest, Langcrest Farm, which has to be seen to be believed. It's a picture, a showplace, beautifully taken care of and exactly suited to its purposes, and on a summer afternoon a delight to study from the back roads around it. You can't help hoping that it won't be swallowed up.

There are many other richly human delights to be contemplated here. Driving west along Highway 37, you find yourself once more in farmland, but land with quite a different tone from that on the eastern section of the river. Here are some country homes, clearly the resorts of rich people, built many years ago on grandiose plans for the old aristocracy of wealth. There are plenty of impressive private docks and some serenely magnificent prospects of the western reaches of the water, the wide calm of Lac des Deux Montagnes beyond, and the hills on either shore of the Ottawa even further away. Perhaps the millionaires built their retreats here so that they could easily intuit any nuance from the nation's capital that might be carried down river on air or current. These views are romantically stately, suggestive of the glories of the old régime, when families like the Gouins or Merciers took care of provincial affairs as they might their own estates, moving in an easy and familiar converse with the federal authority and the directors of industry, a state of affairs long vanished.

Set down among these stately rural retreats are many small

commercial beach resorts, each with a pop stand and a small dock, some with boats for hire, most with picnic tables and accommodations for family outings. On weekends these places are crowded from early morning till long after dark; the hum of light outboard motors dominates the pleasant scene. There is dancing and even an amusement park with roller-coaster and other exciting rides. People play softball, eat hotdogs, chase their children and roll bright coloured balls at them, fall out of punts and skiffs. They come from all over the city to make innocent use of these amenities.

From Monday to Friday afternoon, no business is done, or virtually none. The wife of the proprietor drowses reflectively, leaning against the hotdog counter, selling an occasional candy bar to a child out of school, open for business just because it is summer. The week drifts along like a slow dream; on Thursday the Coca-Cola truck comes by, or the ice-cream delivery. Insects buzz and sometimes sting, a thunderhead builds up westwards over the lake and breaks or doesn't. Time passes.

In the middle of such a week, on an afternoon of great splendour, I drove out that way with my son Dwight, aged five, to get us out of the house and relieve my wife of certain responsibilities. The other kids were down with a mildly infectious summer flu, and there was a certain amount of complaining going on, justifiable under the circumstances. We hoped a day away from the sickroom might keep Dwight from getting it, so I took him along, out the Trans-Canada and up Montée Saint-Charles into Pierrefonds where I turned west on Highway 37, looking for a place to stop and idle away the later afternoon. In a few miles we began to pass refreshment stands and both of us began to think about ice-cream cones.

I dug my hand into my hip-pocket and found that I had about a dollar in change. I rarely carry more than that because I work at home and have everything I need right there. I figured that I had enough for cones and drinks so I pulled into the minute parking lot beside the next booth. Nobody else was parked there. A broken picnic table lay canted to one side next to the car, part of one seat sprung loose and the nails showing. Next to the booth were a couple of empty lard-buckets, shining brassy and slick in the sun. A sign: $1.25 CHAQUE VOITURE.

We waited at the counter till the attendant materialized, a woman of forty, almost certainly the owner's wife. I asked Dwight what he wanted and he chose (after some deliberation) a chocolate cone and a Coke. When he was served, he stood there alternately eating and drinking with unaffected pleasure. My son Dwight is not a demonstrative child, but he has a very pure and clear strain of feeling, not confined to treats and games, and very moving to see. While he enjoyed his treat, I chatted with the lady who had served us and looked curiously at the little park. There wasn't anything specially impressive around, three weathered outbuildings, paths worn through the grass towards the river, a softball diamond with a backstop. I asked about the charges and she explained the sign. 'You can take in five, plus the driver, and stay, and stay as long as you want.'

'How much would it be for the two of us to go in, not for a picnic, just to take a look around?'

She looked at Dwight who was finishing his Coke, smiled at him and got a big grin in return. 'There's nobody here today,' she said, 'why not just leave your car here and walk in with him, no charge. Stay as long as you like. My husband won't mind.'

I hadn't been fishing around for a free admission, and the offer took me aback; it seemed very generous. 'Thanks very much,' I said, 'when the other children are feeling better, perhaps we can bring the whole family.' I paid her for the ice cream and the drink, took my son by the hand and we wandered off together into the park. Dwight was full of questions. He especially wanted to know about the three little wooden buildings which stood about the grounds.

'Two of them are bathrooms,' I said. 'Do you think you need to go?'

'Well, I might try,' he said experimentally.

We went over to the two privies and I pointed out which was for men and which for ladies. He disappeared inside and in a couple of seconds I heard him give a snort of surprise. He emerged laughing.

'There's no water in there, just a hole.'

'It's often that way in the country. Come on, let's look around.'

We examined everything, the tables, the baseball diamond. We walked down to the edge of the river where, in contradistinction to the reeds and garbage to be found eastward, were clean sand and shining stones. It was getting late in the afternoon and though the sun was still high it was sending its beams slantwise along the river from the west, a peaceful sight. We looked out towards a raft bobbing offshore; then I took off his shoes and socks, a bit uneasy about what his mother might think, and let him wade out a few feet.

'When it gets to your knees, stop.'

'Aren't you coming in, Dad?'

'I think I'll keep my feet dry,' I said.

He paddled around for a while, came back in, and I lifted him onto a big rock which stood on the shore to put his shoes on, but his feet were plenty wet and sandy, so I let him walk through the grass barefoot as we went towards the car.

'What's that place, another toilet?' He pointed out the third of the wooden shacks which was bigger than the others, but not very big.

'Let's have a look.' We went over and climbed the steps and found ourselves in a miniature dance hall, a single room about twenty by fourteen with a small raised platform at one side, room enough for three or four musicians. The dance floor was tiny, like a toy; there might have been room for eight couples. On the east side of the shack were screened windows with shutters above for bad weather and winter. Two overhead lights with unshaded bulbs. And in a corner a plugged-in jukebox. Dwight eyed it wistfully, so I pulled out a dime and stuck it in the slot, and the room was filled at once with a great sound.

'Beatles,' shouted my son joyfully, 'yeah, yeah, yeah.' I watched him with amusement; they learn fast these days. Then actuated by an obscure impulse, I began to whirl and caper back and forth in a solo dance; the rhythm was tremendous, the drums prominent.

The record stopped. 'What's that boom, boom, boom, Dad?'

'That's the drums, that's Ringo.'

'Ringo,' he said rapturously. 'Dad, would you buy me drums for Christmas?'

'I'll see about it,' I said, slightly intoxicated. 'Come on and dance some more,' and I fed my last seventy-five cents into the slot, selecting a good loud programme. When the music started I whirled round and round, kicking up my heels, making my son laugh. 'Dad, let me, let me.' So I took him by the hands and showed him how to plant his feet on my insteps. I took great long strides with his cool bare feet pressed against mine. 'More, more!' The music roared, we danced and danced. The floor was worn silky smooth by countless dancing feet, and I slid and glided and turned like some tango-artist in a movie. Then I picked Dwight up in my arms, hugged him, and took a final spin. The last quarter fell into the coin box and there was silence.

Then, 'I love you, Dad.'

'And I love you.'

We didn't get Dwight a drum for Christmas, but chose instead a 'Johnny Seven One Man Army' which had considerable noise potential of its own and seemed an adequate substitute. On Christmas Day, therefore, I left the house in the afternoon, intending to give my ears a rest, without much thinking of where I was headed. I found myself back on the highway towards the little resort where we had danced together: the association of guns, drums, noise, dancing, probably influenced my choice. After an hour's drive I arrived at the refreshment stand and took a careful look around.

The weather that Christmas was very unusual. The temperature was around fifty-five degrees above zero, about thirty-five degrees above normal. It had snowed through early December, right down to the last few days before Christmas, so that there was a thick covering on the ground which the peculiar weather was causing to vaporize in an eerie way. The back river had been frozen since the first of the month, and the ice was giving off a dense steam which became a thick misty pall, almost fog, some feet above the ice. The refreshment stand was deserted. A few black footprints showed here and there in the wet snow covering the park.

I wore uncomfortable but waterproof driving boots, so I risked walking into the grounds. The dance hall was tightly boarded over, the paths undiscoverable, but I pressed on to the shore where I stopped to examine the texture of the ice, to peer into the quiet mist and inhale the vaporous air. My boots were tight and dry but now my trousers were soaking. I couldn't recreate the feeling of our earlier visit.

I gazed towards Lac des Deux Montagnes where, through the mist, the Ottawa hills could just be seen, rounded and palpable, a slightly greyer tone than the intervening air. Two hundred yards off to the west was a solitary black figure, a man in a punt beside a private dock. He held a long black pole with which he jabbed repeatedly at the ice, clearing away some of the softer surface slush from around his property. I considered going to help him, but decided that I'd be wet from head to foot when I got there.

A breeze stirred, slightly thinning the mist, wrapping swirls of vapour around the lonely black figure; all at once the scene composed itself into meaning. Everything in my range of vision was softened or obscured by mist, except those agitated thin black limbs. I raised my eyes to the source of the river, several miles westwards where the lake contracts. Shore, water, air were all enveloped and changed, the city inexistent. Far off northwest, the high hills rose ghostly from the melting ice and snow.

Checklist

1 'The Sportive Centre of Saint Vincent de Paul' was written in Montréal in January 1966 and first appeared in *Around the Mountain: Scenes from Montréal Life*, Toronto: Peter Martin Associates, 1967, pp. 1-20.

2 'Light Shining out of Darkness' was written in Montréal in January 1966 and appeared in *Saturday Night*, April 1966, pp. 30-32.

3 'Bicultural Angela' was written in Montréal in February 1966 and appeared in *The Canadian Forum*, 46 (Aug. 1966), pp. 106-108.

4 'Around Theatres' was written in Montréal in February 1966 and appeared in *Parallel*, 1, No. 3 (July-August 1966), pp. 47-50. First publication includes three drawings by Seymour Segal.

5 'Le Grand Déménagement' was written in Montréal in March 1966 and first appeared in the volume *Around the Mountain: Scenes from Montréal Life*, Toronto: Peter Martin Associates, 1967, pp. 65-79.

6 'Looking Down From Above' was written in Montréal in March 1966 and appeared in *Prism international*, 6, No. 2 (Autumn 1966), pp. 4-13.

7 'One Way North and South' was written in Montréal in April 1966 and appeared in *The Tamarack Review*, No. 41 (Autumn 1966), pp. 82-94.

8 'The Village Inside' was written in Montréal in April 1966 and first appeared in the volume *Around the Mountain: Scenes from Montréal Life*, Toronto: Peter Martin Associates, 1967, pp. 113-126.

9 'A Green Child' was written in Montréal in May 1966 and first appeared in the volume *Around the Mountain: Scenes from Montréal Life*, Toronto: Peter Martin Associates, 1967, pp. 127-139.

10 'Starting Again on Sherbrooke Street' was written in Montréal in May 1966 and appeared in *Parallel*, 1, No. 5, (Nov.-Dec. 1966) pp. 50-54. The story was accompanied by a drawing by Seymour Segal.

11 'Predictions of Ice' was written in Montréal in June 1966 and first appeared in the volume *Around the Mountain: Scenes from Montréal Life*, Toronto: Peter Martin Associates, 1967, pp. 155-166.

12 'The River Behind Things' was written in Montréal in June 1966 and first appeared in the volume *Around the Mountain: Scenes from Montréal Life*, Toronto: Peter Martin Associates, 1967, pp. 167-175.